William Bates

A Funeral-Sermon for the Reverend

holy and excellent divine, Mr. Richard Baxter, who deceased Decemb. 8, 1691 -

with an account of his life

William Bates

A Funeral-Sermon for the Reverend
holy and excellent divine, Mr. Richard Baxter, who deceased Decemb. 8, 1691 - with an account of his life

ISBN/EAN: 9783337780586

Printed in Europe, USA, Canada, Australia, Japan

Cover: Foto ©Andreas Hilbeck / pixelio.de

More available books at **www.hansebooks.com**

A
Funeral-Sermon

FOR THE

Reverend, Holy and Ex-
cellent DIVINE,

Mr. *Richard Baxter*,

Who deceafed *Decemb.* 8. 1691.

WITH

An Account of His LIFE.

By *WILLIAM BATES*, D.D.

LONDON,

Printed for *Brab. Aylmer,* at the *Three
Pigeons* againft the *Royal Exchange*
in *Cornhill.* 1 6 9 2.

To the Right Worſhipfull,
and his much Honoured Friend,

Sʳ *Henry Aſhurſt*, Baronet·

S I R,

YOur *Noble and Conſtant*
Kindneſs to Mr. Baxter
Living, and your Honourable
Reſpect to him Dead, have in-
duced me to inſcribe the follow-
ing Memorial of him to your
Name. He was moſt worthy
of your higheſt Eſteem and Love,
for the firſt Impreſſions of Hea-
ven upon your Soul, were in
Reading his unvalued Book of
the Saints Everlaſting Reſt.
This kindled a mutual Affection
in your Breaſts his Love was

Di-

Directing, Counſelling, and Exciting you to ſecure your Future Happineſs: your Love was Obſervant, Gratefull, and Beneficent to him. The Sincerity and Generoſity of your Friendſhip, was very evident, in your appearing and ſtanding by him, when he was ſo roughly and unrighteouſly handled, by one, who was the diſhonour of this Ages Law ; whoſe Deportment in a high place of Judicature, was ſo contrary to Wiſdom, Humanity, and Juſtice, that there need no foul words to make his Name odious. Of this and your other Favours Mr. Baxter retain'd a dear and laſting Senſe ; and in his dying hours declared, that you had been the beſt

beſt friend he ever had. _He has finiſhed his Courſe, and recei-ved his Crown   _His Name will ſhine longer than his Enemies ſhall bark._

I cannot omit the mentioning, that _Mr._ Boyle _and Mr._ Baxter, _thoſe incomparable_ Perſons _in their ſeveral Studies, and dear Friends, died within a ſhort ſpace of one another._   _Mr._ Boyle _was engaged in the Contemplation of the Deſign and Architecture of the viſible World, and made rare diſcoveries in the ſyſtem of Nature: not for Curioſity and barren Speculation, but to admire and adore the_ Perfections _of the Deity in the Variety, Order,_ Beauty, _and marvellous Artifice of the Creatures_

A 3   _that_

that compoſe this great Univerſe.
Mr. Baxter was converſant in the
inviſible World: his Mind was
conſtantly applied to underſtand
the harmonious Agreement of the
Divine Attributes in the Oeconomy
of our Salvation, and to reſtore
Men to the Favour and Image of
God. They are now admitted into
the inlightned and purified Society
above: where the immenſe Vo-
lumes of the Divine Wiſdom are
laid open, and by one glance of an
eye, they diſcover more perfectly
the Cauſes, Effects, and Concate-
nation of all things in Heaven and
Earth, than the moſt diligent In-
quirers can do here, in a thouſand
years Study, though they had the
Sagacity of Solomon. By the
Light

Light of Glory, they ſee the face of God, and are ſatisfied with his likeneſs for ever. *'Tis a high honour to you, that Mr.* Boyle *and Mr.*Baxter *ſhould by their Laſt Will nominate you amongſt their Executors. It was the Saying of a Wiſe* Roman, Malo divi Auguſti judicium, quam beneficium. *I had rather have the Eſteem of the Emperour* Auguſtus *than his Gifts: for he was an underſtanding Prince, and his Eſteem was very Honourable to a Perſon. That two who ſo excell'd in Wiſdom and Goodneſs, ſhould commit to your Truſt the diſpoſal of their Eſtates for the Uſes of Piety and Charity, is a more noble Teſti-*

mony

mony of their *Eſteem* of your *Pru-dence* and *inviolable Integrity,* than if they had bequeathed to you rich *Legacies.*

It is a *ſatisfaction* to me, that I have complied with *Mr.* Bax-ter's *deſire* in *Preaching* his *Fu-neral-Sermon,* and with yours in *Publiſhing* it. I *ſhall* unfeigned-ly recommend *Your ſelf,* your ex-cellent *Lady,* and *vertuous Chil-dren,* to the *Divine Mercies:* and remain, with great *Reſpect,*

S I R,

Your humble and

faithfull Servant,

William Bates.

A

SERMON

On the DEATH of

Mr. *Richard Baxter.*

Luke 23. 46.

And when Jeſus had cried with a loud Voice, he ſaid, Father, into thy Hands I commend my Spirit.

THE Words are the Pray-er of our Bleſſed Saviour in the Extremity of his Paſſion. His unrighteous and implacable Enemies had nail'd his Body to the Croſs, but they

B   had

had no power over his Spirit, that was ready to take its flight to the Sanctuary of Life and Immortality. This dying Prayer of Chrift is a Pattern for fincere Chriftians : He has invefted them with the Relation of Children of God; and authorifes them by his Example, to commend their departing Spirits to his powerful Love. The Obfervation I fhall unfold and apply, is this :

'Tis the Priviledg of dying Saints, to commend their Spirits into the Hands of their Heavenly Father.

In difcourfing of this, I fhall,

I. Confider the Foundation of this Priviledg.
II. Shew what a bleffed Priviledg this is.
III. Apply it.

I. The

I. The Foundation of this Priviledg is to be confider'd : This is built upon two things.

1. The Relation of God to the Saints.

2. His Perfeftions joined with that Relation.

1. The Relation of God to the Saints. The Title of *Father* is upon feveral Accounts attributed to God.

(1.) He is a Father by Creation : *O Lord, thou art our Fa-* Ifa. 64. *ther : we are the Clay, thou art the Potter, we are the Work of thine Hands.* He formed Man's Body into a Majeftick Figure, becoming his original State, being Lord of the lower World. But in a peculiar manner he is ftiled *the Father of Spirits :* they have a near Alliance, and Refemblance of the Father of Lights, in their intelleftual

Pow-

Powers, and their immortal Nature. From hence it is, the Angels are called *the Sons of God:* They are the eldeſt Off-spring of his Power. *Adam* has the Title of the *Son of God.* And ſince the Fall, Men are called *God's Offspring.* There is an indelible Character of Dignity engraven in the reaſonable Nature by the Hand of God. But ſince Man turn'd Rebel to his Creator and Father, this endearing obliging Relation aggravates his Rebellion, but gives him no Intereſt in the Paternal Love of God, of which he has made a deadly Forfeiture. 'Tis threatned againſt ignorant perverſe Sinners, *He that made them, will not ſave them.*

(2.) Upon the account of external Calling and Profeſſion, there is an intercurrent Relation of Father and Sons between God

Job 2.

Luke 3.

God and his People. Thus the
Pofterity of *Seth* are called *the* Gen. 6.
Sons of God and the entire
Nation of the Jews are fo fti-
led ; *When* Ifrael *was young, I* Hofea 11.
called my Son out of Egypt. And
all that have received Baptifm,
the Seal of the holy Covenant,
and profefs Chriftianity, in this
general Senfe may be called the
Children of God. But 'tis not
the outward Dedication that
entitles Men to a faving Intereft
in God, unlefs they live according to that Dedication. There
are baptized Infidels, as well as
unbaptized. How many every
day fall as deep as Hell, whofe
hopes were high,on the account
of their external Chriftianity.

(3.) God is our Father upon
a more excellent Account, by
Renovation and Adoption. The
natural Man is what St. *Paul*
faith of the voluptuous Widow,

B 3 *dead*

dead while he lives. There is
not only a ceſſation of ſpiritual
Acts, but an utter incapacity to
perform them : he cannot obey
nor enjoy God.   Now the re-
newing of Man is called a Regeneration : Our Saviour tells
*Nicodemus, Verily I ſay unto you,
Unleſſ a Man be born again, he
cannot enter into the Kingdom of
Heaven.*   The reaſon of the
Expreſſion is, becauſe there is a
new Nature, ſpiritual, holy and
heavenly, communicated, different from the carnal, polluted
and earthly Nature, derived
from the firſt *Adam.*   And as
the Relation of a Father reſults
from the communicating a vital
active Principle to another, in
that kind of Life like his own :
ſo God by making us Partakers
of *a Divine Nature, of his Life and
Image,* is ſtiled our Father : *Of*
Jam. 1. 18. *his own Will begat he us, with the*
Word

Word of Truth. And we are said, *to be born again, not of cor-* 1 Pet. 11. *ruptible Seed, but incorruptible, by the Word of God, which liveth and abideth for ever.* By the 25. Divine Influence, the Word of God implants in them such Qualities and Dispositions whereby they resemble God, *are holy, as he is holy, in all manner of Conversation.* They are called *godly,* as they are like him in their Minds, Affections and Actions. And to such God has the Heart and Eye of a Father, to regard and relieve them in all their Exigencies. *Like as a Father* Psal. 103. *pities his Children, so the Lord* 13. *pities them that serve him.*

We are also the Children of God by Adoption. This heavenly Privilege is obtained for us by the meritorious Sufferings of Christ, and is founded in our Union with him. *God sent his*

B 4 *Son,*

Gal. 4. *Son, that he might redeem them*
that were under the Law, that they
might receive the Adoption of Sons.
For his fake we are not only
pardoned, but preferr'd to this
Heavenly Dignity. 'Tis wor-
thy of Obfervation, that the
Degrees of our Redemption
mentioned in Scripture, have
annex'd to them parallel degrees
of our Adoption. Thus when
'tis faid, *We are redeemed from*
the Curfe of the Law, 'tis added,
That we might receive the Adop-
tion of Sons. When 'tis faid,
We are freed from the fervile Spi-
rit of the Law, it follows, *We*
Rom.8.15.*have received the Spirit of Adop-*
tion, whereby we cry, Abba, Fa-
ther. And the Apoftle tells us,
That the redemption of our Bodies from *the bondage of Corrup-*
tion, into the glorious Liberty of
the Sons of God, is our Adopti-
on, that is the manifeftation
of

of it before all the World.

Our Adoption is founded in our Union with Chrift. A Member of Chrift, and a Son of God are the fame : 'Tis therefore faid, *As many as received him, to* Joh. 1. 12. *them gave he Power,* or Privilege, *to become the Sons of God, even to them that believe on his Name.* And *ye are all the Sons* Gal. 3. 6. *of God, by Faith in Jefus Chrift.* This is the vital Band of our Union with Chrift, and invefts us with his Relation to God. When he was to leave the World, he fends this comfortable Meffage to his Difciples ; *Go, tell* Joh. 20. 17 *my Brethren, I afcend to my Father and your Father, to my God and your God.* His Relation has the precedence in Order, Dignity and Caufality. He is God's own Son, in a fenfe infi- Rom. 8. 3. nitely high and proper to himfelf : *To which of the Angels faid* Heb. 1. 5.

he

he *at any time,* Thou art my Son, *to day have I begotten thee ?* The fublimeſt Prophet breaks forth with Wonder, *Who ſhall declare his Generation ?* 'Tis above our Capacity and Conception. It becomes us to acquieſce in what thé Scripture reveals. He is the eternal Word and Wiſdom of God, *the Brightneſs of his Father's Glory.* This is the moſt fit Compariſon : for as Light is productive of Light without any diminution ; ſo the Eternal Father communicated his Eſſence to the Son. In ſhort, God is Chriſt's Father by Nature, and God by Diſpenſation; he is our God as the Author of Nature, and our Father by Adoption.

Before I proceed, it is fit to obſerve the Excellence of the Evangelical Adoption above the Civil Adoption among Men.

(1.) Adop-

Margin notes: Iſa. 53. Heb. 3.

(1.) Adoption is a legal Act in imitation of Nature, for the Comfort of thofe who are without Children. But God had a Son, the Heir of his Love and Glory. His adopting Love is heightned by confidering our Meannefs and Vilenefs : we are but a little breathing Duft, worthlefs Rebels. The Apoftle cries out in a rapture of Admiration and Joy, *Behold what manner of Love the Father hath beftowed upon us, that we fhould be called the Sons of God !* If we confider the natural Diftance between God and us, as he is the Creator, and we are the Works of his Hands, 'tis truly infinite ; but the moral Diftance between the holy righteous God and the guilty polluted Creature, is, if it were poffible, more than infinite : Love inconceivable! That releafes us from

Bon-

Bondage, and adopts us into the
Line of Heaven.   If we admire
any thing of this World in comparifon of it, 'tis a fign we have
no fhare in this Privilege.

(2.) Civil Adoption conveys
no Praife-worthy Qualities into
the Perfon that is adopted.   A
King may adopt one to be his
Son, and the Heir of his Kingdom,   but cannot endow him
with a Royalty of Spirit, with
ruling Wifdom, with Juftice
and Equity, Clemency and
Bounty, with Magnanimity and
Fortitude, that may qualify him
to manage the Scepter.   The
adopted Prince may be of a low
fordid Difpofition, a Slave to
his vile Lufts, and defigning to
enflave others.   But all the a-
dopted Sons of God are divine-
ly renewed; they are purified
from defiling & debafing Lufts,
and are adorn'd with all the
Graces

Graces of the Spirit, that God *is not aſhamed to be called their* Heb. *God and Father, nor Chriſt aſha-* Heb. 2. *med to call them Brethren.* Now from this ſpecial Relation and Intereſt of God in the Saints, there is a ſure Foundation of their Truſt in his ſaving Mer- cy. *David* addreſſes himſelf to God for his preſervation from imminent Danger, *I am thine,* Pſal. 119. *ſave me :* As if his miſcarrying would be a Loſs to God, who had ſo dear a Propriety in him.

I come now to the ſecond thing that encourages the pray- ing Faith of the Saints when they leave the World, to com- mend their Souls to him, His Perfections joined with his Re- lation : His Love inclines, his Truth engages, and his Power enables him to bring them ſafe- ly to Heaven.

1. His

1. His Love. This is the brighteſt Ray of the Deity, the firſt and cleareſt Notion we have of God. St. *John* tells us, *God is Love.* His Love cannot be fully expreſs'd by the deareſt Relations and Affections in Nature. The Relation of Parents, as 'tis moſt deeply implanted in Nature, ſo it implies the moſt cordial, ſtrong and tender Affection. But as God is infinitely greater and better than earthly Parents; ſo he equally excels them, as in his Abilities, ſo in his good Will to his Children. Our Saviour directs us, *Call no Man Father upon Earth, for one is your Father, which is in Heaven :* The Title and Love of a Father is peculiar to him. Our Saviour argues, *If you that are evil, know how to give good things to your Children, how much more ſhall your heavenly Father to thoſe*
that

that ask him ? The Inference is
ſtrong, not only from the Divine Authority of the Speaker,
but from the native Perſpicuity
of the Things: for the Love
of an earthly Father is but an
Infuſion into his Breaſt from the
heavenly Father, and but a faint
reſemblance of his Love. The
Love of a Mother is more tender and endearing than of a Father: Even a fearful Hen will
fly upon Death, to preſerve its
tender Brood from the Devourer: Yet the Love of God to his
Children far excels it. *Can a
Woman forget her ſucking Child?*
What Heart, what Marble is
in her Breaſt ſo incompaſſionate
and unrelenting, as to neglect
her helpleſs Infant? *She may,
but*, ſaith God, *I will never forget
thee*. TheSeraphims, thoſe bright
and unperiſhing Flames, are but
faint and cold, in compariſon
of

of God's Love to his Children.
'Tis obfervable how the
Love of God to them expref-
fes it felf in all the Notions of
Propriety and Precioufnefs, to
make it more fenfible to us.
Exod. 19. They are ftiled *his Treafure, his*
Mal. 3. *Jewels*, the moft precious part
Zech.9. 16 of his Treafure, the *Jewels of
his Crown*, that are the richeft
Jewels. Now *will he throw a-
way* his Treafure, or fuffer the
cruel Enemy to rob him of his
Jewels? Will he not take them
into his fafe Cuftody? 'Tis to
be obferved, that the Efteem
and Affection of God principal-
ly refpects the Souls of his Children: Their Souls have an original Affinity with him in their
Subftance as Spirits: and being
born again of the Spirit, they
are Spirit in their Divine Qualities & Endowments, and more
endear'd to him than by their
firft

firſt Alliance. His tender Care to
preſerve them, will be correſpon-
dent to his Valuation and Love.

Moreover, the Condition
of departing Souls affords another Argument of reliance upon his Love ; for they leave
this viſible World, with all their
Supports and Comforts ; they
are ſtripp'd of all ſenſible Securities : And will he leave them
fatherleſs in ſuch a forlorn and
deſolate State? His Love is expreſs'd by Mercy, Compaſſion,
Pity, melting Affections, that
are moſt tenderly moved when
the beloved Object is in Diſtreſs.
Our Saviour propounds an Argument for dependance upon
the delivering Love of God,
from the Exigence of his People ; *Shall not God deliver his own
Elect*, the Deſignation of Love,
*who cry day and night to him? He
will do it ſpeedily.* Love is ne-
C   ver

ver more ardent and active than in times of Diſtreſs. Therefore when his dying Children are deprived of all their Hopes and dependance upon Creatures, and fly to him for Protection and Relief, will he not hear their mournful Requeſts, and grant their fainting Deſires? When their earthly Tabernacles are ſo ruinous, that they are forc'd to diſlodg, will the Love of a Heavenly Father ſuffer their naked Souls to wander in the vaſt Regions of *the other World, ſeeking Reſt, and finding none?* Certainly he will bring them into his reviving Preſence. If Divine Love be ſo condeſcending, that

Iſa. 57. *the high and lofty One that inhabits Eternity, dwells with the humble and contrite Spirit,* to *revive the Spirit of the Humble,* when they are confin'd to our lowly Earth, we may be aſſur'd, when

that

that Spirit fhall be devefted of
Flefh,he will bring it to Heaven
the Temple of his Glory, to be
with him for ever. 'Tis greater Love for a King to lay a-
fide his State, and dwell in a
mean Cottage with his Favou-
rite, than to receive him into
his Palace, and communicate to
him of his rich Abundance.
'Tis another moft comfortable
Confideration, that the Love of
God is unvariable towards his
Children : His Love is the fole
moving Caufe of our filial Relation to him : *Of his own Will* James.
he begat us by the Word of Truth.
His Soveraign free Love was the
Principle of his electing any to
the Dignity of being his Children: This Love is as unchangeable as free; and Election that
proceeds from it, is as unchangeable as his Love. What can in-
duce him to alter his Affection

towards them? For such is the
perfection of his Knowledg, that
he can never be surprized by a
sudden new Event, that may
cause a change in his Mind and
Will. He foresaw all the Sins
of his People, with their provo-
king Aggravations. Now if the
foresight of them did not hinder
his electing Love in its rise, can
they frustrate its end, the bring-
ing of them to Glory?

Besides, we may argue from
what his Love has done for his
Children, to what he will do:
He has given his Son and Spirit
to them, the surest Signs of his
Love, if we consider the unvaluable Excellence of the Gifts,
and the Design of the Giver.

The Son of God is the most excellent Gift of his Love, as un-
deserved, as he was undesired:
And from hence the Apostle argues, *He that gave his Son for*

us all, how much more will he with him give us all things? Bleſſed God! What richer Evidence, and more convincing Demon-ſtration can there be of thy Love? *Will he not with him give us all things?* The Inference is direct and concluſive, with re-ſpect to temporal and eternal Things. He will give to his Children in the preſent World, whatever his Wiſdom, in con-junction with his Love, ſees good for them. To illuſtrate this by a low and familiar In-ſtance; If a Mother beſtows upon her Daughter rich Jewels for her Marriage-Ornaments, will ſhe deny her Pins to dreſs her? And we may as ſtrongly argue, that with his Son he will give us eternal Bleſſings. Will he give us the Tree of Life, and not permit us to eat of the Fruit of it? What was the deſign of

C 3 his

his Counſel and Compaſſion, in
giving his Son to be a Sacrifice
for us, but to reſtore us to his
Favour? The Apoſtle reaſons
ſtrongly, *If when we were Ene-*
mies, we were reconciled to God
by the Death of his Son, much
more being reconciled, we ſhall be
ſaved by his Life. He has paid
our Ranſom, and revers'd the
Sentence of Condemnation a-
gainſt us; and it invincibly follows, he can more eaſily accom-
pliſh our Happineſs in Heaven.
If Love juſtify a Sinner, it will
glorify a Saint.

And as the Gift of the Son,
ſo the moſt precious Gift of the
Spirit to God's Children, to
make them holy and heavenly,
is the moſt certain ſign of his
Love to them. The Apoſtle
in the fulleſt expreſſion ſpeaks
of it; *God who is rich in Mercy,*
for his great Love wherewith he
has

*has loved us, even when we were
dead in Sins, quickned us together
with* Christ : *By Grace ye are sa-
ved.* Sanctification is the effect
of *rich Mercy, great Love,* and
saving Grace. The Children of
God are seal'd by the Holy Spirit to the Day of Redemption :
that Seal diftinguifhes them
from the obftinate and polluted
World, and ratifies the convey-
ance of eternal Life to them.
The Spirit is ftiled the *Earneft
of the Inheritance.* His dwelling
in the Saints by his fanctifying
and comforting Operations, is
an Earneft of their dwelling
with God in his Sanctuary a-
bove. From hence the Apoftle
propounds a ftrong Argument
to affure the Saints, upon their
leaving this World, of their reception into Heaven ; *Now he
that hath wrought us for the felf-
fame thing, is God ;* and the

Al-

Almighty always obtains his End : *who hath also given us the earnest of his Spirit.* Holineſs is the Morning-Star of the great Day ; Grace is the Preparative and Aſſurance of Glory : For altho the Saints are in themſelves mutable, and while there remains Corruption within, and a tempting World without, are liable to falling away, yet the free and powerful Love of God that revived them when dead, will preſerve them living; that which raiſed them from the Grave, will prevent their relapſing into it. *The Gifts of God are without Repentance.* How triumphantly does the Apoſtle Rom. 8. expreſs his Confidence, *Who ſhall ſeparate us from the Love of God ? Shall Tribulation, or Diſtreſs, or Perſecution, or Famine, or Nakedneſs, or Peril, or Sword ?* Theſe are the moſt powerful Terrors that

that the perverſe World, in com-
bination with the Devil, can
make uſe of to conſtrain us to
deſert the Service of God ; but
they are vain. *Nay, in all theſe*
things we are more than Conque-
rors, through him that loved us :
For I am perſwaded, that neither
Death, nor Life, nor Angels, nor
Principalities, nor Powers, nor
Things preſent, nor Things to
come, nor Height, nor Depth,
nor any other Creature, ſhall be
able to ſeparate us from the Love
of God, that is in Chriſt Jeſus
our Lord. This bleſſed Aſſurance of the Apoſtle is not rais'd
from his extraordinary Privile-
ges, not from the apparition of
Angels to him, nor his rapture
to Paradiſe, nor ſpecial Revela-
tions, but from the Love of God
in Chriſt Jeſus our Lord, that
everlaſtingly embraces all his
Children. Briefly, in that God
has

has given his Son to die for us, and his Spirit to live in us, his Son to purchase and prepare Heaven for us, his Spirit to prepare us for Heaven, a dying Saint may with bleſſed Tranquillity commend his Soul into God's Hands.

I have more particularly conſidered the Fatherly Love of God, what a ſtrong Security it affords to his Children, that he will never leave them, in that no Point requires and deſerves more Confirmation, and weight of Argument to preſs it down into our diſtruſtful Hearts.

2. The Divine Truth affords a ſtrong Security to the Children of God, to commend their Souls to him at laſt. Truth is an Attribute as eſſential and dear to God as any of his Perfections. And in the Accompliſhment of our Salvation, he ordered all

things

things becoming to his Wifdom, that is for the illuftration of all his principal Attributes, and accordingly defign'd the Glory of his Truth equally with the Honour of his Mercy. Thus he declares to his chofen People, *Know therefore that the Lord thy* Deut. 7. 9. *God, he is God, the faithful God, which keepeth Covenant and Mercy, with them that love him, and keep his Commandments.* The Attribute that is fet next to the Deity, as moft facred, is the *Faithful God* ; and that further exprefs'd, *keeping Covenant and Mercy* ; for he delights in fulfilling his Promifes, as in the freeft Acts of Mercy. The Pfalmift breaks forth with the affectionate Praifes of thefe Attributes, *I will worfhip towards* Pfal.138.2 *thy holy Temple, and praife thy Name for thy loving Kindnefs and thy Truth: for thou haft magnified*

nified thy Word above all thy Name. His Word here immediately fignifies his Promife, that has its rife from his loving Kindnefs, and its performance from his Truth. This he magnifies both with refpect to the matter of his Promifes that are exceeding great and precious, and the fulfilling them above all that we can ask or think. God cannot *repent or lie*; his Counfels are unretractable, from the Immutability of his Nature; his Promifes are infallible, from his Fidelity: they are as unchangeable as the Sun and Stars in their appointed Courfes; nay, more ftable than the Centre: *for Heaven and Earth fhall pafs away,* but not a tittle of his Promifes, and our Hopes be unfulfilled. If the Frame of Nature were diffolved, it would be no lofs to God, who is glorious and bleffed in

Jer.31.35.

in his own Perfections: but if
his Promiſes fail, the Honour of
his Truth would be impair'd
and blemiſh'd. The Pſalmiſt
ſaith, *Thoſe that know thy Name,
will truſt in thee:* Thoſe who
know the Creature, its Levity,
Mutability and Mortality, will
be diſcourag'd from truſting in
it ; but thoſe who know the e-
ternal Conſtancy of God in his
Nature and Promiſes, will ſe-
curely rely upon him.

 Now the Promiſes, the Decla-
rations of God's Love, without
which we cannot have any ſolid
and ſuſtaining Hope in our
Death, aſſure us of God's receiving the ſeparate Spirits of his
Children. There was a conſtant
clearneſs, tho not in that degree
of Light as ſince the appearance
of Chriſt, of the Happineſs of
the departed Saints. Dying *Jacob* breaks forth with a lively
Hope,

Gen. 49. 18. Hope, *O Lord, I have waited for thy Salvation.* *Job* says, *Tho he kill me, yet will I truſt in him* ; that is, for his Almighty Mercy in the next State. The Pſalmiſt expreſſes his Confidence, Pſal.73.24 *Thou wilt guide me by thy Counſel, and receive me into thy Glory.* After the ſafe conducting him through a World of Troubles and Temptations, he would bring him to Heaven, a Place of equal Purity and Glory. *David* when he was in preſſing Peril, Pſal.31. 5. addreſſes to God, *Into thy Hands I commend my Spirit*, to be preſerved as a precious Depoſitum ; *thou haſt redeemed me, O Lord God of Truth.* His Aſſurance is built on God's Right and Title to him, *Thou haſt redeemed me,* and his everlaſting Fidelity. The Apoſtle ſpeaks 2 Cor.5. 1. with full aſſurance, *We know that if our earthly Houſe of this*

Taber-

Tabernacle be diſſolved, we have a Building of God *eternal in the Heavens.* And, *we are confident, I ſay, rather to be abſent from the Body, and preſent with the Lord.* St. *Peter* encourages Chriſtians when ſurrounded with Death, *to commit their Souls to him* : 1 Pet. 4. 1. *Wherefore let them that ſuffer according to the* Will *of* God, *commit the keeping of their Souls to him in wel-doing, as unto a faithful Creator.* He encourageth them to encounter Death in its moſt formidable Pomp, by conſidering their Souls ſhall be ſafe for ever, upon the account of God's Right and Intereſt in them, and his Fidelity : he has an original Right in them by the firſt Creation, as they are intellectual immortal Spirits in their Nature, but a nearer and more eſpecial Right by a new and nobler Creation, as they are

re-

renewed Spirits, made like to him in his Holiness, the moſt Divine Perfection. The Relation of Creator implies his omnipotent Love, and the Attribute of Faithful, his eternal Love declar'd in his Promiſes. There can never be the leaſt cauſe to charge him with Inſincerity or Inconſtancy. The

Pſal. 5.

Favour of God is round about the Righteous as a Shield: And his

Pſal. 89.

Faithfulneſs is round about him, that he is always ready to perform his Promiſe to them. They may ſafely truſt the worth of their Souls, and the weight of Eternity with him, who has ſaid, *he will never leave them, nor forſake them.*

Beſides, the Promiſe of a Reward to the obedient Children of God, is ſecur'd not only by his Fidelity, but the declar'd Equity of his Proceedings in his

his final Judgment. 'Tis a Re-
gality invefted in the Crown of
Heaven to difpenfe Rewards:
Whoever comes to God, muft be- Heb.11.6.
lieve that he is, and that he is a
rewarder of them that diligently
feek him. His Being and rewar-
ding Bounty are the Foundati-
ons of Religion. 'Tis true, fuch
is the Diftance between God
and the Creature, and the eternal Obligations of it to God,
that it can challenge nothing
from God, as due to its Merit.
Juftice unqualified with Bounty
and Clemency, owes nothing to
the moft excellent Obedience of
the Creature, tho innocent. But
fince the Fall, our beft Works
are defective and defiled, and
want Pardon ; and our heavieft
Sufferings are but light in the
Ballance, againft the exceeding
Weight of Glory. But the Apoftle tells the Theffalonians, *It is*

D *a*

a righteous thing with God to re-
compenfe Tribulation to them who
trouble you : and to you who are
troubled, reft with us. Confider
them in the Comparifon ; 'Tis
becoming his governing Juftice
to punifh the unrighteous Per-
fecutors, and reward his faithful Seryants who fuffer for his
Glory. Now the prefent.Life
is the Day for our Work, as our
Saviour faith, *I muft do the Work*
of him that fent me, while 'tis cal-
led to Day : And at Death, the
Spirit returns to God that gave it,
in order to Judgment, either fatal or favourable, according to
the tenor of Mens good Works,
and the defert of their bad. The
Promife is *to them, who by pati-*
Rom. 2. *ent continuance in wel-doing, feek*
for Glory, and Honour, and Im-
mortality, they fhall obtain eter-
nal Life. Our Saviour encourages his fuffering Servants, *Be*
faith-

faithful to the Death, and I will give you the Crown of Life. The compleat Reward is referved to the great Day of universal Recompences, when the Sons of God by Regeneration, shall be the Sons of a glorious Refurrection. But the righteous Judg will give a prefent Reward at the end of the Day, to all that with unfainting Perfeverance have perform'd his Work. Our Saviour tells us, that all who wrought in the Vineyard, receiv'd their Rewards *in the last Hour of the Day*: The Parallel is inftructive, that when the Night of Death comes, the Reward will be difpens'd. There is a Law recorded concerning the paying Wages to thofe who were hir'd, that it fhould be in the end of the Day ; that it fhould not be detain'd *all Night with thee until the Morning.* The

Luke 20: 35:

Mat. 20. 9:

Deut. 24: 15:

D 2   Allu-

Allufion is very congruous, that God will fulfil his own Law to his Sons that ferve him. The Reward fhall not abide with him the long dark Interval, the Night, wherein their Bodies fleep in the Grave, till the Morning of the Refurrection. Our Saviour promifed the dying Penitent, *To day fhalt thou be with me in Paradife.* *The End of our Faith* is immediately attended *with the Salvation of the Soul:* The Labour of Faith being finifh'd, is productive of the beatifick Vifion in the State of Light and Glory. The Sum is, That the Children of God, who have by conftant Converfation fincerely endeavoured to pleafe and glorify him, may with an entire Refignation commit their Souls to his Hands, as if an Angel were fent from Heaven to them in their dying Agonies, with the

the comfortable Meſſage, that
they ſhould preſently be with
God.

3. The Divine Power, in con-
junction with Love and Truth,
is the Foundation of our ſecure
dependance upon God in our
laſt Hours. This Conſideration
is abſolutely neceſſary for our
ſure Truſt : For Love without
Power is ineffectual, and Power
without Love of no comfortable
Advantage to us. The Apoſtle
gives this reaſon of his chearful
and couragious Sufferings in the
Service of God, *For I know in
whom I have believed, and am*   2 Tim. 1.
*perſwaded he is able to keep what I
have committed to him, till that
Day.* His Faith reſpected the
Promiſes of God concerning his
Salvation, which are infinitely
ſure, the Divine Power being
alſufficient to fulfil them. The
precious Depoſitum that is com-
D 3   mitted

mitted to his dear Care, he can and will preferve inviolate. The Father of fincere Believers, is *the Lord of Heaven and Earth,* who by his Word, without the leaft ftrain of his Power, made the World, and preferves it from falling into Confufion. 'Tis the Effence of Faith, to af-fure us of God's Almighty Mercy to all that have the true Chara&ers of his Children, that are qualified for his Salvation. Our Redeemer joins the two Relations of *our Father and our God;* the gracious and the glorious Relation are infeparable. Now the Love of our heavenly Father engages the Power of our God, that we fhall want nothing to fecure our Happinefs, that is within the objed of Omnipotence.

I fhall infift no further upon the Confideration of the Divine
Power,

Power, becaufe it will return under fome of the following Heads of Difcourfe.

II. The Bleffednefs of this Privilege is to be unfolded. This will appear by confidering,

Firft, What is the Depofitum, the Thing that is intrufted in God's Hands.

Secondly, What is implied in his receiving of it.

In anfwer to the firft; 'Tis the Soul, the more excellent and immortal Part of Man, that is commended to God's keeping.

1. 'Tis our more excellent Part in its Nature and Capacity. Man is a compounded Creature, of a Body and a Soul : the Body in its Original and Refolution is Earth ; the Soul is of a divine Defcent, a fpiritual Subftance, and in the Nobility and Perfections of its Nature,

D 4   but

but *a little lower than the Angels:* 'tis *the vile Body, but the precious Soul.*

In its Capacity it incomparably excels the Body; for the Body lives & moves in the low Region of the Senses, that are common with the Worms of the Earth; but the Soul in its Understanding and Desires, is capable of Communion with the blessed God, of Grace and Glory. From hence it is, that the whole World can't make one Man happy; for the Ingredients of true and compleat Happiness are the Perfection and Satisfaction of the Soul. The Apostle tells us, *The less is blessed of the greater.* Can the World bring Perfection to Man, that is so incomparably short of his Imperfection? Our Saviour assures us, *the Gain of the whole World cannot recompense the Loss of one Soul.* There

There is a vaſt Circuit in our
Deſires, and all the Lines ter-
minate in the Centre of Bleſſedneſs. Can the World give ſincere Satisfaction to them? *So-*
lomon who was as rich and high
as the World could make him,
has left an everlaſting Teſtimony of the Vanity of tranſient
Things, from his experimental
Obſervation, and the Direction
of the Holy Spirit: So he be-
gins and ends his Sermon, *Va-* Ecclef. 1.
nity of Vanities, all is Vanity ; ſo 1. & 12.8.
vain and vexing, that we ſhall
not only be weary of them, but
of this Life, wherein we uſe Ecol.1.17.
them. Can the Creature make
us happy, when their Empti-
neſs, and Anguiſh annex'd to it,
makes our Lives miſerable?
The World cannot ſatisfy our
narrow Senſes: *The Eye is not*
ſatisfied with ſeeing, nor the Ear
with hearing, much leſs the infinite

nite Defires of our fupreme Faculties. Thofe who are now inchanted with its Allurements, within a little while will fee through its falfe Colours. As when one awakes, all the pleafant Scenes of Fancy in his Dream vanifh ; fo when the Soul is awakened in the End of Life, *the World and the Lufts thereof pafs away,* and the remembrance of them.

I fhall add further ; What clearer Evidence can we have of the worth of the Soul, than from God's Efteem, the Creator of it? Now when God forefaw the Revolture of our firft Parent, that brought him under a double Death in one Sentence, temporal and eternal, and that all Mankind was defperately loft in him, then his compaffionate Counfels were concerning his Recovery : His Love and Wifdom

dom' accorded to contrive the
Means to accomplifh our Redemption, by the Death of his
incarnate Son : *We are not re-* ¹ Pet. 1;
deemed with Silver and Gold, but
with the precious Blood of Chrift,
as a Lamb without fpot and ble-
mifb. Of what value is a Soul
in God's account, that he bought
with his own Son's Blood, the
moft facred Treafure of Heaven ? We may fay for the Honour of our Redeemer and our O anima !
own, that which the Angels erige te,
tanti vales;
cannot, we were fo valued by *Aug.* in
God himfelf, that his Son be- Pfal.103.
came Man, and died on the
Crofs for the Salvation of our'
Souls. I fhall only mention a-
nother Evidence and Effeɛ of
God's valuation of our Souls,
that is, *the eternal Weight of*
Glory, which exceeds all the
Thoughts of our Minds, and
Defires of our Hearts. What'
                                        are

are all the Kingdoms and Plea-
sures of the World, in compa-
rison of that Bleſſedneſs God
has prepar'd *for thoſe who love
him?* Now the Soul that is in-
eſtimably precious, and ſhould
be moſt dear to us, is ſecured
from Danger, when received by
God's Hands.

2. The Soul is our immortal
Part. The Body is compounded
of jarring Principles, frail and
mortal : A Caſualty or Sickneſs
diſſolves the vital Union, and
it falls to the Duſt. But the
Soul is a Spirit by Nature, and
immortal by its inherent Pro-
perty. Its ſpiritual Operations
perform'd without the miniſtry
of the Senſes, (the Eye of the
Mind contemplates its Objects,
when the Eyes of the Body are
clos'd) demonſtrate its ſpiritual
Nature : for the Being is the
Root of its working, and conſe-
quently

quently that it exifts indepen-
dently upon the Body : But of
this we have the cleareft affurance in the Scripture.   This is
another demonftration that prefent Things cannot make us
happy, for they forfake us the
firft ftep we take into the next
World, and then the Soul enters
into Happinefs or Mifery equally eternal.   The Immortality
of the Soul, and the Immutability of its State, are infeparable
then; for the prefent Life is the
time of our Work, the next is
of Recompences according to
our Works. *If we die in the
Lord,* the Confequence is infallible, we fhall live with him for
ever : If we die in our Sins, we
fhall not be received by his
merciful Hands, but fall into
his bottomlefs Difpleafure. And
of what concernment is it to
have our Souls with God in that
                              infinite

infinite and incomprehenfible
Duration ? All the Meafures of
Time, Days and Weeks, Months
and Years, and Ages, are fwal-
low'd up in that invifible Depth,
as the Rivers that pour into
the Sea, are fwallowed up
without any overflowing of
its Waters. The Dove that
Noah let out of the Ark, as a
Spy to difcover whether the
Deluge was abated, found not
a Place to reft on; but after many Circuits in the Air, it re-
turned to the Ark. If our
Thoughts take wing, and mul-
tiply Millions of Millions of
Ages, we cannot reft in any
Computation, for there remains
after all an entire innumerable
Eternity.

Secondly, I will confider more
particularly what is contained
in this bleffed Privilege: The
reception of the Soul into God's
Hands,

Hands, implies three things.
1. Entire Safety.
2. Heavenly Felicity.
3. 'Tis a certain Pledg of the reviving of the Body, and its reunion with the Soul in the State of Glory.

1. Entire Safety. After Death the feparate Soul of a true Believer immediately paffes through the airy and Ethereal Regions to the higheft Heaven, the Temple of God, the native Seat and Element of bleffed Spirits. The Air is poffefs'd by Satan with his Confederate Army, who are Rebels to God, and Enemies to the Souls of Men : he is ftiled *the Prince of the 'Power of the* Ephef. 2. *Air :* He often raifes Storms and Tempefts, difcharges Thunder and Lightning, the woful Effects of which are felt in the lower World. The Numbers, the Strength, and the Malice of the

the evil Angels to the Souls of
Men, render them very terrible:
We may conjecture at their
Number, from what is related
Mark 5. in the Gospel, that *a Legion
possess'd one Man.* They are
superiour Spirits to Man, and
tho stripp'd of their moral Excellencies, Holiness, Goodness
and Truth, yet retain their natural Power at leaft in great degrees. Their Malice is un-
quenchable. 'Tis faid of the
Devil, *He goes about like a roar-
ing Lion, feeking whom he may de-
vour.* All the Joy thofe ma-
lignant Spirits are capable of, is
the involving the Souls of Men
in their defperate Calamity.
And tho they know their oppo-
fing God will increafe their
Guilt and Torment, yet their
Diligence is equal to their Malice, to feduce, pervert and ruin
Souls for ever. Now when the
Saints

Saints die, all the Powers of Darknefs would, if poffible, hinder the afcenfion of their Souls to God. What *David* complains of his cruel Enemies, is applicable in this cafe, *Their Souls are among Lions* ; and if deftitute of divine Prefervation, the Danger would be the fame ; as if a little Flock of Lambs were to encounter with a great number of fierce Lions, or fiery Dragons. Anger fets an edg upon Power, and makes a Combatant but of equal Strength to overcome. How dangerous then would the Condition be of naked Souls, oppos'd by overmatching Enemies, armed with Rage againft them ? How eafily would they hurry them to *the Abyfs*, the Den of Dragons, the Prifon where loft Souls are fecur'd to the Day of Judgment ?

But all the Potentates of Hell

E are

are infinitely inferiour to God : they are reftrain'd and tortur'd by the Chains of his powerful Juftice : a Legion of them could not enter into the Swine without his permiffion, much lefs can they touch *the Apple of his Eye.* That black Prince with all his infernal Hoft cannot intercept one naked Soul from arriving at the Kingdom of Glory. Our Saviour affures us, *None is* John 10. *able to pluck them out of his Father's Hands.* The Lord Chrift our Head and Leader, having vanquifh'd in his laft Battel on the Crofs, Principalities and Powers, made his triumphant Afcenfion to Glory : Thus his Members having overcome their fpiritual Enemies, fhall by the fame Almighty Power be carried through the Dominions of Satan, *in the fight of their Enemies,* (tormented with the remembrance

membrance of their loft Happinefs, and Envy that humane
Souls fhould partake of it) to
the Place of God's glorious Refidence.

I fhall alfo obferve, that as
the Lord is a God of Power, fo
he is a God of Order, and ufes
fubordinate Means for the accomplifhment of his Will. Our
Saviour has reveal'd, that the
Angels tranfport the feparate
Souls of the Righteous to Heaven : Thofe glorious Spirits,
who always behold the Face of
God, fuch is their exact Obedience to him, and perfect Love
to his Children, that they dif-
dain not to protect his little ones
in this open State. They *rejoice* Mat.18.10
at the Converfion of Sinners, at
their firft entrance into the Way
of Life, and with tender watch-
fulnefs encompafs them here,
never withdrawing their pro-

E 2　　　tecting

tecting Prefence, till they bring
them to their celeftial Country,
and refign their Charge to the
Lord of Life. How fafe are the
departed Saints, when convey'd
through Satan's Territories by
the Royal Guard of Angels *that*
excel in ftrength?

    2. Heavenly Felicity. The
receiving of holy Souls into
God's Hands, is introductive
into his Prefence, which is both
a Sanctuary to fecure us from
all Evil, and a Store-houfe to
furnifh us with all that is good.
The Lord is a Sun and a Shield :
he is to intellectual Beings, what
the Sun is to fenfitive, communicates Light and Life, and Joy
to them. *In his Prefence is ful-*
Pfal.16.11 *nefs of Joy, at his right Hand*
are Rivers of Pleafure for ever.
All that is evil and afflicting, is
abolifh'd : all that is defirable,
is conferr'd upon his Children.

               A

A glimpfe or reflected Ray of his reconciled and favourable Countenance, even in this lower World, infufes into the Hearts of his Children a *Joy unfpeaka-ble and glorious :* a tafte of the Divine Goodnefs here, caufes a difrelifh of all the carnal Sweets, the dreggy Delights which natural Men fo greedily defire. And if the faint Dawn be fo reviving and comfortable, what is the Brightnefs of the full Day? None can underftand the Happinefs that refults from the full and eternal fight of God's Face, and the fruition of his Love, but thofe who enjoy the Prefence of God in perfection. His Goodnefs is truly infinite ; the more the Saints above know it, and enjoy it, the more they efteem it, and delight in it. His compleat and communicative Love fatisfies the immenfe Defires of

E 3   that

that innumerable Company of
bleffed Spirits that are before his
Throne : there is no Envy, no
Avarice, no Ambition in that
Kingdom, where *God is all in all.*

The Divine Prefence is an e-
ver-flowing Fountain of Felicity. The continual reflection
upon this, makes Heaven to be
Heaven to the Bleffed : their
Security is as valuable as their
Felicity : they are above all
danger of lofing it. Methinks
the belief of this fhould caufe
us, as it were with Wings of
Fire, with moft ardent Defires
to fly to the Bofom of God, the
alone Centre of our Souls, where
we fhall reft for ever.

3. The reception of the Soul
into Heaven is a certain Pledg
of the Refurrection of the Body,
and its re-union with the Soul
in the State of Glory. The Covenant of God was made with
the

the entire Perfons of Believers :
therefore under the Law the facred Seal of it was in their Flefh.
To be the God of Promife to
them, implies his being a bleffed Rewarder to them. Our Saviour filences the Sadduces, who
disbeliev'd the Refurrection,
from the tenour of God's Covenant, *I am the God of* Abraham,
and Ifaac, *and* Jacob, which Title he was pleafed to retain after their Death ; *Now God is not
the God of the Dead, but of the
Living.* The immediate Inference from thence is, that their
Souls did actually live in Bleffednefs, and that their Bodies,
tho dead to Nature, were alive
to God with refpect to his Promife and Power. If we confider that the Divine Law binds
the outward Man as well as the
inward, and that during the
time of our Work and Trial
E 4 here,

here, our Service and Sufferings
for the Glory of God are from
the concurrence of the Soul and
Body, it will appear that the
Promife of the Reward belongs
to both, and that the receiving
of the Soul into Heaven, is an
earneft of our full Redemption,
even that of the Body. 'Tis
true, there is no vifible Difference between the Bodies of the
Saints and of the Wicked here;
they are fick with the fame Dif-
eafes, and die in the fame manner. As 'tis with Trees in deep
Winter, when they are covered
with Snow, we cannot diftin-
guifh which are abfolutely dead
and deftin'd to the Ax and Fire,
and which retain their Sap, and
will be fruitful and flourifhing
in the returning Year: fo the
dead Bodies of the Godly and
Ungodly, to external appearance, are alike: But what a vaft
diffe-

difference will be between them in the next World ! The Bodies of the Ungodly, in conjunction with their Souls, fhall be caft into the Lake of Fire; the Bodies of the Godly refumed by their Souls, fhall enjoy a full and flourifhing Happinefs for ever.

The Application.

1. This may inform us of the contrary States into which dying Perfons immediately pafs: The Children of God refign their Spirits to the Hands of their gracious Heavenly Father, but Rebels and Strangers to God, fall *into the Hands of* a revenging Judg. Could we fee the attending Spirits that furround fick Perfons in their laft Hours, what a wonderful Impreffion would it make upon us? A Guard of glorious Angels.

convey

convey the departed Saints to
the Bofom of God's Love, and
the Kingdom of his Glory. But
when the Wicked die, a Legion
of Furies fieze upon their ex-
pected Prey, and hurry them to
the infernal Prifon, from whence
there is no redemption.

How many Rebels and open
Enemies to God are in the Pale
of the Chriftian Church? They
will loudly repeat, *Our Father*
which art in Heaven, notwithftanding the impudent and pal-
pable Atheifm of their Lives:
they live as if they were independent, and not accountable
to him *who will judg the World*
without refpect of Perfons. The
more ftrict his Commands are,
the Contempt of them is more
vifible. Our Saviour's Prohibi-
tion is peremptory, *I fay unto*
you, Swear not at all : but how
many make no more confcience
of

of Swearing than they do of
Speaking, and pour forth Oaths
of all fafhions and fizes. We
are feverely forbid all degrees of
Impurity, in the Look, in Words,
or in Wifh; yet how many
without reflection or remorfe,
continue in the deepeft Polluti-
ons! We are commanded to
live foberly in this prefent World;
yet how many indulge their
fwinifh Appetites, and debafe
themfelves even below the Beafts
that perifh. And as the fenfual
Appetites are notorioufly pre-
dominant in fome, fo the angry
Appetite is tyrannous in others.
Pride, Wrath, Revenge, poffefs
the Breafts of many: How often for a flight, or but reputed
Injury, they are fo fir'd with
Paffion, that their hot Blood
cannot be fatisfied without the
cold Blood of their Enemies.
In fhort, many live in fuch open
defi-

defiance of the Divine Law, as
if there were no God to fee and
punifh their Sins, or as if they
would make a trial whether he
will be true to his Threatning,
and revenge their bold Impie-
ties : They· are partly worfe
than Brutes ; for having an underftanding Faculty, a Principle of Reafon, they fubmit it to
Senfe : and partly worfe than
Devils ; for as the Devils, they
rebel againft God, and yet not,
as they, tremble in their Rebellion.   Now when Death is
ready with its cold Hands to
clofe their Eyes, and Confcience awakes out of its Slumber,
what Horrors feize upon them !
They are ftripp'd of their carnal Securities, the Creature cannot help them, and the Creator.
will not. They have been Enemies to that Love that made
them and preferv'd them, and,
not-

notwithftanding their violent
Provocations, has fpar'd them
fo long. They have rejected
that infinitely condefcending
and compaffionate Love, that fo
tenderly befeech'd them to be
reconciled to God, as if it were
his Intereft to fave them. Whi-
ther will they fly from their
Judg? What can refcue them
from inftant and irrecoverable
Mifery? Can they hope that
Mercy will be their Advocate?
Their Condemnation is fo righteous, that Mercy cannot difpenfe with it. *'Tis a fearful
thing to fall into the Hands of
the living God*, who lives for
ever, and can punifh for ever.
Who *knows the Power of his
Wrath?* 'Tis boundlefs beyond
all our Thoughts and Time. O*
take notice of this with Terror,*
all ye that forget God, leſt he tear Pfal. 50.
you in pieces, and there be none to
deliver!   Others

Others are not fo vifibly difobedient as notorious Sinners,
but are as really.   You may fee
their Picture in the difobedient
Son, mentioned by our Saviour
Matth. 21. in the Gofpel, who *when his Fa-*
28, 30. *ther commanded him to go work in*
the Vineyard, anfwered, I go, Sir,
and went not.   'Tis true, they
perform the external part of
fome Duties, and abftain from
the grofs acts of fome Sins, but
'tis with an exception and a re-
ferve.   A Duty that is contrary
to their carnal Appetites and
Intereft, they will not perform ;
a Sin that bribes them with Pro-
fit or Pleafure, a temperamental
Sin, they will not part with.
Now any indulged habitual
Luft *is not the Spot of God's*
Children, but denominates the
Sinner a Child of the Devil :
for tho the Saints till they are
devefted of frail Flefh, have
their

their Allays, and cannot be exempt from the relicks of Sin;
yet the Divine Nature communicated to them, is oppofite to
every Sin, and is an active Principle to fubdue Sin.

And from hence S. *John* tells
us, *He that is born of God, cannot fin,* that is, deliberately and
habitually : Such Sinners,tho in
the Hour of Death they may
addrefs with all the applying
Titles, *Our Father, and our God,*
fhall ever be excluded from his
facred and faving Protection.

2. Let us ferioufly confider
whether we are of this fpiritual Progeny, the Children of
God, not only in Title, but in
Reality.   The Inquiry is of infinite moment ; for all the Promifes and Priviledges of the
Gofpel are annex'd to this Son-
fhip : This fecures us from *the
Wrath to come,* and entitles us

to

to the eternal Inheritance; *Fear*
Luke 12. *not, little Flock, 'tis your Father's
good Pleasure to give you the
Kingdom.* This Inquiry is very
useful to calm and quiet the
troubled Saints, and to awaken
unregenerate Persons out of
their confident Dream of their
good State. Many sincere Chri-
stians are infinitely concern'd
whether they are the Children
of God; of this their Tears and
Fears give abundant evidence.
The reasons of their Doubts are
partly the Jealousy of their own
Hearts, which are naturally *deceitful above all things*, and most
deceitful to a Man's self; and
partly from the consequence of
the Deceit: for knowing the
inestimable value of this Privilege, *to be the Sons of God*, and
that if they are deceived in it,
they are undone for ever, they
are anxiously thoughtful about
it.

it. But carnal Perſons who are
not acquainted with the Hypo-
criſy of their Hearts, nor duly
underſtand the excellence of the
Privilege, eaſily believe what
they coldly deſire. And the
great deceiver of Souls is equally ſubtile to varniſh what is evil
with the falſe colours of Good,
and to conceal what is good under the appearance of Evil.
From hence it is, that many
tender-ſpirited Chriſtians are
timorous, and full of unquiet
Agitations all their Lives : and
many who have but a ſhew and
fair pretence of Religion, are
undiſturb'd and hopeful, till at
laſt they fall from their ſuppo-
ſed Heaven and high Hopes, into the Abyſs of Miſery.

This Trial will be moſt clear
and convincing, by repreſenting
from Scripture the inſeparable
Properties and Characters of the
F   Chil-

Children of God, that diftin-
guifh them from all that are in
the State of unrenewed Nature.
The Apoftle tells fincere Chriftians, *The Spirit it felf witnef-*
fes with our Spirits, that we are
the Children of God.   Here is a
Confent and Agreement of thofe
Witneffes, in whom are all that
is requifite to give value to their
Teftimony.   For the Spirit of
God, fuch is his unerring Knowledg, *who fearches the deep things*
of God, and fuch is the abfo-
lute Sanctity of his Nature, that
he can neither deceive nor be
deceived, fo that his Teftimony
is infinitely fure, and of more
worth than the concurrent Teftimony of Heaven and Earth,
of Angels and Men. The other
Witnefs is the renewed Confcience, that is acquainted with
the Aims and Affections of the
Heart, as the Apoftle faith,
Who

*Who knows the things of a Man,
save the Spirit of a Man?* This
Faculty reflects upon our Actions, and the Principles of them:
to this Faculty is referr'd the
decision of our spiritual State;
If our Hearts condemn us not of   1 John 3.
any allowed Sin, *then have we
Peace towards God.* From the
consent and agreement of these
Witnesses, there is a blessed Af-
surance of our Evangelical Son-
ship, that overcomes all our
Fears. Now this Testimony
is rational and argumentative,
from the discovery of those
Graces that constitute a Person
the Child of God. I will make
the Inquiry concerning the
Grace of Faith and of Love,
which are the vital Bands of our
Union with Christ, the principal Fruits of the sanctifying
Spirit, and the Symptoms of
Salvation.

(1.) The Grace of Faith is ex-
Joh. 1. 12. prefs'd in Scripture by *receiving
of Chrift :* this anfwers to God's
offer of him to our acceptance in
the Gofpel.   It receives him entirely in his Perfon and Natures,
as the incarnate Son of God ;
and in his Office, as *a Prince*
Acts 5. 31. *and Saviour, to give Repentance
and remiffion of Sins.*   This receiving Chrift implies an Act
of the Underftanding and the
Will ; the Underftanding af-
fents to the Truth of the Divine Revelation, that Chrift
crucified is an alfufficient Saviour ; and the Will clofes with
the Terms of it, *that he will
fave to the uttermoft all that obey
him :* From hence it follows,
that reliance upon him, and a
fincere refolution to obey him,
are neceffarily included in faving Faith.   This Scripture-
Account diftinguifhes between
that

that fubftantial Faith that is
proper to the elect Children of
God, and the Shadow of it in
the Unregenerate; the one is
the intimate and active Principle of Obedience, the other is
a dead Affent without Efficacy,
a mere Carcafs and Counterfeit
of Faith. A fincere Believer
as fervently defires to be faved
from the Dominion and Pollution of his Sins, as from the
Guilt and deadly Malignity : a
carnal Man defires an Intereft
in Chrift as a Saviour, that he
may fecurely enjoy his Lufts.

The crafty and curfed Ser-
pent deceives Men to their ruine, by citing Scripture, and
mifapplying it. The Promife
is fure, *Whoever believes, fhall
be faved* ; and he eafily per-
fwades them they are Believers. 'Tis ftrange to aftonifhment, that Men who have Rea-

fon and Underftanding, fhould prefume in a high degree of the prefent Favour of God, and their future Happinefs, as if they were his dear Children, when their Enmity againft his holy Name and Will is evident in their Actions.

We can never have too firm a dependance on God's Promife, when we are qualified for that Dependance. *Come out from a-mong them, and be ye feparate, faith the Lord ; and touch not the unclean thing, and I will re-ceive you, and will be a Father to you, faith the Lord Almighty.* Faith that purifies the Heart and Converfation, invefts us with this bleffed Privilege, and all the faving Mercies annex'd to it.

2 Cor. 6. 17, 18.

(2.) From the fpiritual Re-lation between God and Belie-vers, there naturally and necef-farily

farily refults a fincere, dutiful,
child-like Love to him, correfpondent to his beneficent and
fatherly Love to them : This
God indifpenfably requires, and
fpecially delights in ; *Thou lo-*
veſt Truth in the inward Parts. Pſal. 51.
Filial Obedience is infeparable
from filial Love in its Reality :
For this is the Love of God, that 1 Joh. 5. 3.
we keep his Commandments. Our
Saviour diftinguifhes between
fincere Lovers of him, and pre-
tended, that *they who love him,*
keep his Commandments ; *but* John 14.
they who love him not, keep not 23, 24.
his Commandments.

The Obedience that fprings
from Love to God, is uniform,
refpeĉts all his Commands : for
the two filial Affeĉtions, an ardent Defire to pleafe God in all
things, and an ingenuous Fear
of difpleafing him in any thing,
are infeparably joined with

our Love to him.

The Obedience that proceeds from Love, is free and voluntary, from Inclination as well as Duty. How paſſionately does the holy Pſalmiſt expreſs his Affection, *O how I love thy Law!* In the Covenant of Grace, God Heb. 8. 10. promiſes to *write his Law in the Hearts of his Children :* not only in their Minds and Memories, but to endear it to their Affections. There is much difference between ſervile and conſtrain'd Obedience, and filial choſen Obedience, as between the Motion of a living Man from the Soul, the inward Spring of Life, and the Motion of an Image or Statue from forcible Weights and Wheels.

From filial Love proceeds godly Sorrow, if at any time by Careleſneſs and Surprize, or an over-powering Temptation,

on, his Children do what is of-
fenfive and odious in his fight.
When they confider their unkind
and unthankful Returns for
his Mercies, they look to their
Heavenly Father with Grief
and Shame, and down upon
themfelves with Abhorrence
and Indignation : They are
wounded with the fting of that
Expoftulation, *Do ye thus re-
quite the Lord, O foolifh People* Deut. 32.6
*and unwife? Is he not thy Father
who bought thee?*

From filial Love proceeds a
Zeal for his Glory ; *If I be a Father, where is my Honour?* A
Child of God is dearly concer-
ned that his Name be reveren-
ced and magnified, his Laws
be obferved, his Worfhip main-
tained, that his Intereft be ad-
vanced in the World. He has
a burning Zeal againft Sin and Pfal. 69.
prefumptuous Sinners. The
Pro-

Prophet *Elijah* ſays, *I have been jealous for the Lord of Hoſts : for the Children of* Iſrael *have forſaken thy Covenant, and thrown down thine Altars.* Thoſe who with an indifferent Eye ſee the Cauſe, the Truth, the Intereſt of God depreſs'd in the World, do renounce the Title of his Children.

From the Relation to God as his Sons, proceeds a ſincere fervent Love to all the Saints. St. ₁Joh.5. 1. *John* infers, *Every one that loveth him that begat, loves him that is begotten.* Grace is not leſs powerful in producing cordial mutual Affections between the Children of the ſame Heavenly Father, than the ſubordinate Endearments of Nature. Notwithſtanding the civil Diſtinction between them, ſome high and rich, others mean and poor, yet there is a ſpiritual Equa-

Equality ; the loweſt Saints are Princes of the Blood-Royal of Heaven. *To him that has waſhed us from our Sins in his Blood, and* Revel. 1. *made us Kings and Prieſts to God, be Glory for ever.*

The filial Relation to God inclines and encourages all ſincere . Chriſtians to reſign themſelves, even in their moſt afflicted Condition, to the Wiſdom and Will of God. Our Saviour meekly yielded up himſelf to his cruel Enemies, upon this Conſideration, *The Cup which my Father* Joh. 18. 11 *has given me, ſhall I not drink it ?* The Saints in imitation of Chriſt, and upon the ſame Ground, entirely reſign themſelves to the Divine Diſpoſal ; for their Heavenly Father loves them better than they can love themſelves.

Finally, The filial Relation to God is productive as of lively

ly Hopes, fo of ardent Defires
to be with him. Love makes
them to efteem Communion
with him here in his holy Ordi-
nances, as the Joy of their
Lives. The Pfalmift when ba-
nifh'd from the Tabernacle,
breaks forth in his impatient De-
Pfal. 43. fires, *When fhall I come and ap-*
pear before God? that is, in the
Place where he communicates
his Grace to thofe that worfhip
him. But our Father is in Heaven as his Throne, and moft
glorioufly exhibits himfelf to
his Saints there. The Earth is
the Element and Refidence of
carnal Men, of their Souls as
well as their Bodies: They defire their *Inheritance may be on*
this fide Jordan, and are content
to leave the Heavenly *Canaan*
to thofe who like it. But thofe
who *are born from above,* defire
to be diffolved, that they may
be

be in their Father's Houfe, and his reviving Prefence for ever.

3. Let us be perfwaded to prepare for the reception of our Souls in the next World. The prefent Life is a Paffage to Eternity, and 'tis fo fhort and fading, fo uncertain and hazardous, that 'tis our principal Wifdom without delay to fecure our Souls in the future State. Our Saviour fays, *I muft work the Work of him that fent* John 9. 4. *me while it is Day: the Night cometh when no Man can work. Now is the accepted Time, now is the Day of Salvation.* 'Tis our indifpenfable Duty and main Intereft now, *to work out our own Salvation with fear and trembling.* In the ftate of Death there is an Incapacity to do any thing in order to Salvation: *There is no Work nor Wifdom in the Grave:* and all the Offers of Sal-

Salvation ceaſe for ever. The Sufferings of the Son of God are not a Ranſom for Sinners in that State: *He reconciled things in Earth and in Heaven*, but not things in Hell. The Golden Scepter is extended to none there, the Holy Spirit ſtrives with none, they are without the Reſerves of Mercy. The Guilt of Sin remains in its full Obligation, the Pollution of Sin in its deepeſt Die, and the Puniſhment of Sin in its Extremity for ever.

O what Folly is it, or rather Frenzy, not to provide for our Souls in their greateſt Exigence! Common Reaſon inſtructs us, knowing our own Weakneſs, to commit our Treaſure to the cuſtody of our Friends, which we cannot otherwiſe keep from our Enemies; eſpecially to ſuch a Friend as can and will preſerve

ferve it for our Ufe and Advantage. The Soul is our Jewel
above all Price, 'tis our Wifdom
to fecure it out of all danger:
Let us therefore commit it to
the fafe and fure Hands of our
Heavenly Father, otherwife we
cannot preferve it from the infernal Spirits, the Robbers and
Murderers of Souls.

The wife Preacher denoun-
ces a fearful Evil, *Wo be to him
that is alone when he falleth*; *for* Eccl.4.10.
*he hath not another to help him
up.* In all the Senfes of falling,
Death is the greateft Fall: the
High, the Honourable, the
Rich, fall from all their State;
and Men of all Degrees are for-
faken of all their carnal Comforts and Supports. If then the
folitary Soul has not a God to
receive, fupport and comfort it,
how woful is its Condition!
Methinks the apprehenfion of
this

this fhould ftrike a Terror fo
deep into the Hearts of Men,
that they fhould be reftlefs till
they have fecur'd a Retreat for
their departing Souls.

For this end let us, according
to the earneft Advice of St. *Pe-*
2 Pet. 3. *ter, be diligent, that we may be*
found of him in Peace, without.
fpot, and blamelefs.

The Lord Jefus is the only
Peace-maker of the righteous
and holy God to Sinners. The
Judg of this World is flaming
with Wrath, and terrible in
Vengeance to Sinners that appear before his Tribunal out of
Chrift. We fhall for ever be
excluded from his bleffed Communion, without the Mediator
reftore us to his Favour. Our
Col. 1. 20. Reconciliation only is by *Re-*
demption in his Blood. The Cha-
Ifa. 53. *ftifement of our Peace was upon*
him. He is *the Lord our Righte-*
oufnefs,

oufnefs, by whom alone we can
ftand in Judgment. *God was in*
Chrift reconciling the World to him-
felf. There is now an Act of Ob-
livion offer'd in the Gofpel to all
that come *to God by him.* We
have fure Salvation in his Name :
But we muft with confenting
Wills, clofe with him as our Lord
and Life. The firft Gofpel preach'd
by the Angel after his coming into the World, declares, *There*
was born in the City of David *a*
Saviour, Chrift the Lord. We
muft not feparate between Chrift
the Saviour, and Chrift the Lord;
between his Salvation and his Dominion. God indifpenfably requires we fhould refign our felves
to his Son as our King, and rely
upon him as our Prieft to atone
his Difpleafure. If we thus receive him, he will reflore us to
the Favour and Peace of God,
eftablifht in an everlafting Covenant. G How

How tenderly and compaſſio-
nately does the great God invite
Sinners to re-enter into his Favour, *to acquaint our ſelves with
him, and to be at peace!* His Em-
*baſſadours in his Name, and in
Chriſt's ſtead beſeech them to be reconciled to God.* But their perverſe Spirits would *have God reconciled to them,* that they might
be exempt from Puniſhment ; but
are *unwilling to be reconciled to
him,* to part with their Luſts. In
ſhort, reconciliation with God ne-
céſſarily infers defiance with Sin.
* Te that love the Lord hate Evil.* If
Men do not ceaſe their Rebellion,
there is no ſhadow of hope to
obtain the Divine Favour.

*Do ye provoke the Lord to Jea-
louſie, are you ſtronger than he?*
Jealouſie is the moſt ſenſible and
ſevére Affection. As 'tis with a
Town taken by ſtorm, all that
are found in Arms are without
Mer-

Mercy cut off; fo all that at Death are found with the *weapons of unrighteoufnefs,* their unrepented unforfaken Sins about them, muft expect *Judgment without Mercy.*

Laftly, Let the Children of God be encouraged with Peace and Joy to commend their Souls to him. Let rebellious Sinners tremble with deadly Fear upon the brink of Eternity; but let the Saints, with a lively Hope, enter into the Divine World.

If Men poffefs their Treafure with Joy and Jealoufie, and guard it with vigilant Care, will not God preferve his deareft Treafure, the Souls of his Children committed to his Truft?

Can Love forfake, can Truth deceive, can Almighty Power fail? Will a Father, a heavenly Father, be without Bowels to his own Off-fpring? No, he cannot deny

himfelf : he is readieft to relieve,
when they are in diftrefs.

Old *Simeon* is a leading Example to Believers : after he had
embraced Chrift in his Armes,
how earneftly did he defire his
Diffolution? *Lord, now letteft thou
thy Servant depart in peace, for
mine eyes have feen thy Salvation.*
St. *Stephen* in the midft of a fhowr
of Stones, with a bleffed Tranquillity, makes his dying Prayer, *Lord Jefus receive my Spirit.*
If the Fears of humble Souls arife
in that hour, becaufe they have
not the Confpicuous marks of
God's Children, the Graces of the
Spirit in that degree of Eminency,
as fome Saints have had : Let
them confider, there are different
Ages among the Children of God :
fome are in a ftate of Infancy and
Infirmity ; others are more Con-
firm'd : but the relation is the
fame in all, and gives an intereft

in

in his promifed Mercy. The weaknefs of their Faith cannot fruftrate
God's faithfulnefs. 'Tis the Sincerity, not the Strength of Grace,
that is requifite to Salvation. If
Faith be fhaking *as a bruifed reed*,
and but kindling as *the fmoaking
flax*, it fhall be victorious. O
'that thefe powerfull Comforts
may encourage dying Chriftians
to commend their Souls with Ar-
dency and Affurance to God, their
Father, and Felicity.

I have now finifht my Difcourfe upon the Text, and fhall
apply my felf to fpeak of the o-
ther Subject, the Reverend Mr.
Richard Baxter, that Excellent Inftrument of Divine Grace, to recover and reftore fo many revol-
ted Souls to God, out of the Em-
pire of his Enemy: or in the A-
poftles Language, *to tranflate them
from the Kingdom of Darknefs, in-*

to the Kingdom of his dear Son. I
am senfible, that in fpeaking of
him I fhall be under a double
Difadvantage : For thofe who perfectly knew him, will be apt to
think my Account of him to be
fhort and defective, an imperfect
Shadow of his refplendent Vertues : others who were unacquain-
ted with his extraordinary Worth,
will from Ignorance or Envy be inclin'd to think his juft Praifes to be
undue and exceffive. Indeed if
Love could make me eloquent, I
fhould ufe all the moft lively and
graceful Colours of Language to a-
dorn his Memory : but this Confideration relieves me in the Con-
fcioufnefs of my Difability, that
a plain Narrative of what Mr.
Baxter was, and did, will bee a
moft noble Eulogy : and that his
fubftantial Piety no more needs
artificial Oratory to fet it off,
than refined Gold wants Paint

to

to add .Luftre and Value to
it.

I fhall not fpeak of his Paren-
tage, and his firft Years: but I
muft not omit a Teftimony I receiv'd concerning his early Piety.
His Father faid with Tears of Joy
to a Friend, my *Son* *Richard* I
hope was fanctified from the
Womb : for when he was a little
Boy in Coats, if he heard other
Children in play fpeak profane
Words, he would reprove them
to the Wonder of thofe that
heard him.

He had not the Advantage of
Academical Education : but by
the Divine Bleffing upon his rare
Dexterity and Diligence, his Sacred Knowledge was in that Degree of Eminence, as few in the
Univerfity ever arrive to. Not
long after his Entrance into the
Miniftry the Civil War began,
and the Times rain'd Blood fo

G 4　　　long,

long, till the languiſhing State of
the Kingdom, was almoſt deſpe-
rate and incurable. How far he
was concern'd as a Chaplain in
the Parliament's Army, he has
publiſht an Account, and the reaſons of it.

After the War, he was fixt at
Kederminſter. There his Miniſtry
by the Divine Influence, was of
admirable Efficacy. The Harveſt
anſwer'd the Seed that was ſow-
ed. Before his coming, the Place
was like a Piece of dry and barren Earth, onely Ignorance and
Profaneneſs as Natives of the Soil
were rife among them ; but by
the Bleſſing of Heaven upon his
Labour and Cultivating, the Face
of Paradiſe appear'd there in all
the Fruits of Righteouſneſs. Many
were tranſlated from the ſtate of polluted Nature, to the ſtate of Grace;
and many were advanc'd to higher
degrees of Holineſs. The bad were
chang'd

chang'd to good, and the good to better. Conversion is the Excellent Work of Divine Grace : the Efficacy of the Means is from the Supreme Mover. But God usually makes those Ministers succesfull in that Blessed Work, whose principal Design and Delight is to glorifie him in the saving of Souls. This was the reigning Affection in his Heart ; and he was extraordinarily qualified to obtain his End.

His Prayers were an Effusion of the most lively melting Expressions, and his intimate ardent Affections to God ; from the *abundance of his Heart his Lips spake*. His Soul took Wing for Heaven, and rapt up the Souls of others with him. Never did I see or hear a holy Minister addrels himself to God with more Reverence and Humility, with respect to his glorious Greatness ; never
with

with more Zeal and Fervency correfpondent to the infinite Moment
of his requefts; nor with more Filial Affiance in the Divine Mercy.

In his Sermons there was a
rare Union of Arguments and Mo-
tives to convince the Mind and
gain the Heart : All the Fountains
of Reafon and Perfwafion were
open to his difcerning Eye. There
was no refifting the Force of his
Difcourfes without denying Reafon and Divine Revelation. He
had a marvellous Felicity and Co-
pioufnefs in fpeaking. There was
a noble Negligence in his Stile :
for his great Mind could not
ftoop to the affected Eloquence
of Words : he defpis'd flafhy Oratory : but his Expreffions were
clear and powerful, fo convincing
the Underftanding, fo entring into the Soul, fo engaging the Affections, that thofe were as deaf
as Adders, who were not *charm'd*
by

by ſo wiſe a Charmer. He was a-
nimated with the Holy Spirit, and
breath'd Celeſtial Fire, to inſpire
Heat and Life into dead Sinners,
and to melt the obdurate in their
frozen Tombs. Methinks I ſtill
hear him ſpeak thoſe powerfull
Words: *A Wretch that is condemn'd* His Ser-
to dy to Morrow cannot forget it : mon be-
And yet poor Sinners, that con- fore the
tinually are uncertain to live an Houſe of
Hour, and certain ſpeedily to ſee Commons
the Majeſty of the Lord to their 1660.
unconceivable Joy or Terror, as
ſure as they now live on Earth,
can forget theſe things for which
they have their memory : and
which one would think ſhould
drown the matters of this World,
as the report of a Canon does a
Whiſper, or as the Sun obſcures
the pooreſt Glo-worm. O won-
derfull ſtupidity of an unrenewed
Soul ! O wonderfull folly and di-
ſtractedneſs of the ungodly ! That
ever

ever Men can forget, I say again, that they can forget, Eternal joy, Eternal Woe, and the Eternal God, and the place of their Eternal unchangeable Abodes, when they stand even at the door; and there is but the thin Vail of Flesh between them and that amazing sight, that Eternal gulph, and they are daily dying and stepping in.

Befides, his wonderfull diligence in Catechizing the particular Families under his Charge, was exceeding ufefull to plant Religion in them. Perfonal inftruction, and application of Divine Truths, has an excellent advantage and efficacy to infinuate and infufe Religion into the Minds and Hearts of Men, and by the Converfion of Parents and Mafters to reform whole Families that are under their immediate direction and government. While he was at *Keder-*

derminfler he wrote and publifht
that accomplifht Model of an E-
vangelical Minifter, ftyled *Gildas*
Salvianus, or the Reform'd Paftor:
In that book, he clears beyond all
cavil, That the Duty of Minifters
is not confin'd to their Study and
the Pulpit, but that they fhould
make ufe of opportunities to in-
ftruct Families within their Care,
as 'tis faid by the Apoftle, that he
had kept back nothing from his
Hearers *that was profitable, but*
had taught them publickly, and
from houfe to houfe. The Idea of
a faithfull Minifter delineated in
that book, was a Copy taken from
the Life, from his own zealous
Example. His unwearied induftry
to do good to his Flock, was anfwer'd by Correfpondent Love and
Thankfulnefs. He was an Angel
in their Efteem. He would often
fpeak with great Complacence of
their dear Affections: and a little
before

before his Death, faid, He believ'd
they were more Expreffive of
kindnefs to him, than the Chriftian Converts were to the Apoftle *Paul*, by what appears in
his Writings.

While he remain'd at *Keder-
minfter*, his Illuftrious Worth was
not fhaded in a Corner, but dif-
pers'd its Beams and Influence
round the Countrey. By his Counfel and Excitation, the Minifters
in *Worcefterfhire*, Epifcopal, Presbyterian and Congregational were
united, that by their Studies, Labours, and Advice, the Doctrine
and Practife of Religion, the
Truths and Holinefs of the Gofpel
might be preferved in all the Chur-
ches committed to their Charge.
This Affociation was of excellent
ufe, the ends of Church-govern-
ment were obtain'd by it : and it
was a leading Example to the Minifters of other Counties. Mr.
Bax-

Baxter was not above his Brethren Minifters, by a Superiour Title, or any fecular advantage, but by his divine endowments and feparate excellencies, his extraordinary wifdom, zeal, and fidelity : he was the Soul of that Happy Society.

He continued among his beloved people, till the year 1660. then he came to *London*. A while after the King's Reftoration, there were many Endeavours us'd in order to an Agreement between the Epifcopal and Presbyterian Minifters. For this end feveral of the Bifhops elect, and of the Minifters, were call'd to attend the King at *Worcefter*-Houfe : there was read to them a Declaration, drawn up with great wifdom and moderation, by the Lord Chancellor the Earl of *Clarendon*. I fhall onely obferve that in reading the feveral parts of the Declaration, Dr. *Morley*

ley was the principal manager of the Conference among the Bishops, and Mr. *Baxter* among the Ministers: and one particular I cannot forget ; it was desir'd by the Ministers, that the Bishops should exercise their Church Power with the counsel and consent of Presbyters. This limiting of their Authority was so displeasing, that Dr. *Cosins*, then elect of *Durham*, said, If your Majesty grants this you will Unbishop your Bishops. Dr. *Reynolds* upon this produced the Book, entituled, *The Portraiture of his Sacred Majesty in his Solitude and Sufferings*, and read the following Passage : *Not that I am against the managing of this Presidency and Authority in One Man by the joint Counsel and Consent of many Presbyters: I have offer'd to restore that, as a fit means to avoid those Errors, Corruptions and Partialities, which are incident to*

to any One Man : alſo to avoid Ty-
ranny, which becomes no Chriſtians,
leaſt of all Church-men. *Beſides,*
it will be a means to take away
that burthen and odium of affairs,
which may lie too heavy on one
Man's ſhoulders, as indeed I think
it did formerly on the Biſhops here.
The good Doctor thought, that
the Judgment of the King's afflicted and inquiring Father would
have been of great moment to
incline him to that temperament :
but the King preſently repl'ed,
All that is in that Book is not Goſpel.
My Lord Chancellor prudently
moderated in that matter, that
the Biſhops, in weighty Cauſes,
ſhould have the aſſiſtance of the
Presbyters.

Mr. *Baxter* conſidering the
ſtate of our affairs in that time,
was well pleaſed with that Declaration : He was of *Calvin's* mind,
who judiciouſly obſerves, upon
H our

our Saviour's words, That *the Son of Man shall send forth his Angels, and they shall gather out of his Kingdom all things that offend: Qui ad extirpandum quicquid displicet præpostere festinant, antevertant Christi judicium, & ereptum Angelis officium sibi temere usurpant. They that make too much haste to redress at once all things that are amiss, anticipate the Judgment of Christ, and rashly usurp the Office of the Angels.* Besides, that Declaration granted such a freedom to Conscientious Ministers, that were unsatisfied as to the Old Conformity, that if it had been observed, it had prevented the dolefull Division succeeded afterward. But when there was a motion made in the House of Commons, that the Declaration might pass into an Act, it was oppos'd by one of the Secretarys of State, which

was

was a fufficient Indication of the
King's averfenefs to it.

After the Declaration there were
many Conferences at the *Savoy*
between the Bifhops and fome
Doctors of their Party, with Mr.
Baxter and fome other Minifters,
for an Agreement, wherein his
Zeal for Peace was moft confpicuous: but all was in vain. Of
the Particulars that were debated,
he has given an account in Print.

Mr. *Baxter*, after his coming
to *London*, during the time of Liberty, did not neglect that which
was the principal Exercife of his
Life, the preaching the Gofpel,
being always fenfible of his duty
of faving Souls. He Preacht at
St. *Dunftans* on the Lord's-days in
the Afternoon. I remember one
inftance of his firm Faith in the
Divine Providence, and his Fortitude when he was engaged in

his Miniftry there. The Church was Old, and the People were apprehenfive of fome danger in meeting in it : and while Mr. *Baxter* was Preaching, fomething in the Steeple fell down, and the noife ftruck fuch a terror into the People, they prefently, in a wild diforder, run out of the Church : their eagernefs to hafte away, put all into a tumult : Mr. *Baxter*, without vifible difturbance, fat down in the Pulpit : after the hurry was over, he refum'd his Difcourfe, and faid, to compofe their Minds ; *We are in the Service of God to prepare our felves, that we may be fearlefs at the great noife of the diffolving World, when the Heavens fhall pafs away, and the Elements melt in fervent heat ; the Earth alfo, and the Works therein fhall be burnt up.*

After

After the Church of St. *Dun-stans* was pull'd down in order to its re-building, he removed to *Black-Fryars*, and continued his preaching there to a vaſt Con-courſe of Hearers, till the fatal *Bartholomew*.

In the Year 1661, a Parliament was call'd, wherein was paſt the Act of Uniformity, that expell'd from their publick Places about two thouſand Miniſters. I will onely take notice concerning the Cauſes of that Proceeding, that the Old Clergy from Wrath and Revenge, and the young Gentry from their ſervile Compliance with the Court, and their Diſtaſte of ſeri-ous Religion, were very active to carry on and compleat that Act. That this is no raſh Imputation upon the ruling Clergy then is e-vident, not onely from their Con-

H 3   cur-

currence in paffing that Law, for
Actions have a Language as convincing as that of Words, but
from Dr. *Sheldon* then Bifhop of
London their great Leader; who
when the Lord Chamberlain *Man-
chefter*, told the King, while the
Act of Uniformity was under de-
bate, *that he was afraid the Terms
of it were fo rigid, that many of
the Minifters would not comply
with it ;* he replyed, *I am a-
fraid they will.* This Act was
paft after the King had engaged
his Faith and Honour in his Declaration from *Breda, to preferve
the Liberty of Confcience inviolate,*
which promife open'd the way for
his Reftorat on; and after the
Royalifts here, had given publick
Affurance, that all former Animo-
fities fhould be buried, *as Rubbifh
under the Foundation of a Univer-
fal Concord.* Mr. *Baxter* was in-
volv'd with fo many Minifters in
this

this Calamity, who was their brighteſt Ornament, and the beſt Defence of their righteous, though
oppreſſed Cauſe: Two Obſervati-
ons he made upon that Act and
our Ejection.

The one was, that the Miniſters were turned and kept out
from the publick Exercife of their
Office, in that time of their Lives,
that was moſt fit to be dedicated
end employed for the Service and
Glory of God, that is between
thirty and ſixty Years, when their
intellectual and inſtrumental Faculties were in their Vigour. The
other was in a Letter to me after
the Death of ſeveral Biſhops who
were concurrent in paſſing that
Act, and expreſt no Sorrow for
it: his words were, *for ought I
ſee, the Biſhops will own the turn-
ing of us out, at the Tribunal of
Chriſt, and thither we appeal.*

H 4   After

After the Act of Uniformity had taken its effect, in the Ejection of so many Ministers, there was sometimes a Connivance at the private Exercise of their Ministry, sometime publick Indulgence granted, and often a severe Prosecution of them, as the Popish and Politick Interest of the Court varied. When there was Liberty, Mr. *Baxter* applyed himself to his delightful Work, to the great Advantage of those who enjoyed his Ministry. But the Church-Party oppos'd vehemently the Liberty that was granted. Indeed such was their Fierceness, that if the Dissenting Ministers *had been as wise as Serpents, and as innocent as Doves,* they could not escape their deep Censures. The Pulpit represented them as seditiously disaffected to the State, as obstinate Schismaticks, and often the *Name of God was not onely taken*

in

in vain, but in violence, to autho-
rife their hard Speeches, and har-
der Actions againſt them. Some
drops of that Storm fell upon
Mr. *Baxter,* who calmly ſubmit-
ted to their injurious dealings. I
ſhall ſpeak of that afterward.

In the Interval, between his De-
privation and his Death, he wrote
and publiſht the moſt of his Books,
of which I ſhall give ſome account.

His Books, for their number
and varfety of Matter in them,
make a Library. They contain
a Treaſure of Controverſial, Ca-
ſuiſtical, Poſitive and Practical Divinity. Of them I ſhall relate
the Words of one, whoſe exact
Judgment, joyn'd with his Moderation, will give a great value 'to
his Teſtimony; they are of the
very Reverend Dr. *Wilkins,* after-
wards Biſhop of *Cheſter :* he ſaid
that Mr. *Baxter* had *cultivated e-
very Subject he handled ;* and *if he*
had

had lived in the Primitive Times, *he had been one of the Fathers of* *the Church.* I ſhall add what he ſaid with admiration of him ano- ther time, *That it was enough for* *one Age to produce ſuch a Ierſon* *as* Mr. Baxter. Indeed, he had ſuch an amplitude in his Thoughts, ſuch vivacity of Imagination, and ſuch ſolidity and depth of Judg- ment, as rarely meet together. His inquiring Mind was freed from the ſervile dejection and bondage of an implicit Faith. He adher'd to the Scriptures as the perfect Rule of Faith, and ſearcht whe- ther the Doctrines received and taught were Conſonant to it. This is the duty of every Chri- ſtian according to his capacity, eſpecially of Miniſters, and the neceſſary means to open the Mind for Divine Knowledge, and for the advancement of the Truth. He publiſht ſeveral Books againſt the Papiſts

Papifts with that clearnefs and ftrength, as will Confound, if not Convince them. He faid, *he onely defir'd Armies and Antiquity againft the Papifts : Armies*, he caufe of their bloody Religion fo often exemplified in *England*, *Ireland*, *France* and other Countries. However they may appear on the Stage, they are always the fame perfons in the Tyring-room : their Religion binds them to extirpate Hereticks, and often over-rules the milder inclinations of their nature : *Antiquity*, becaufe they are inveigled with a fond pretence to it, as if it were favourable to their Caufe : but it has been demon-ftrated by many learned Prote-ftants, that the Argument of Antiquity is directly againft the principal Doctrines of Popery, as that of the Supremacy, of Tranfubftantiation, of Image-worfhip, and others.

He

His Books of the Reasonableness of the Christian Religion. He has wrote several excellent Books against the impudent Atheism of this loose Age. In them he establishes the fundamental Principle, upon which the whole Fabrick of Christianity is built; that after this short uncertain life, there is a future state of happiness or misery equally Eternal, and that Death is the last irrevocable step into that unchangeable state. From hence it follows by infallible Consequence, that the reasonable Creature should prefer the interest of the Soul before that of the Body, and secure Eternal life. This being laid, he proves the Christian Religion to be the onely way of fallen Man's being restor'd to the favour of God, and obtaining a blessed Immortality. This great Argument he manages with that clearness and strength, that none can refuse assent unto it, without denying the infallible Princi-

Principles of Faith, and the evident Principles of Nature.

He alfo publifht fome warm Difcourfes, to Apologize for the Preaching of Diffenting Minifters, and to excite them to do their Duty. He did not think that Act of Uniformity could difoblige them from the Exercife of their Office. 'Tis true, Magiftrates are Titular-Gods by their Deputation and Vicegerency, but fubordinate and accountable to God above. Their Laws have no binding force upon the Confcience, but from his Command ; and if contrary to his Law, are to be difobeyed. The Minifters Confecrated to the Service of God are under a moral perpetual Obligation of Preaching the faving Truths of the Gofpel, as they have opportunity. There needs no miraculous Teftimony of their Commiffion from Heaven, to authorize·the doing their ordinary Duty: In

In some points of modern Controverſie he judiciouſly choſe the middle way, and adviſed young Divines to follow it. His reverence of the Divine Purity, made him very ſhy and jealous of any Doctrine that ſeem'd to reflect a blemiſh and ſtain upon it. He was a clear aſſerter of the ſoveraign Freeneſs, and infalliible Efficacy of Divine Grace in the Converſion of Souls. In a Sermon reciting the Words of the Covenant of Grace, *I will put my fear into their hearts, and they ſhall not depart from me ;* he obſerved the Tenor of it was, *I will, and you ſhall.* Divine Grace makes the rebellious Will obedient, but does not make the Will to be no Will. By the Illumination of the Mind, the Will is inclin'd to Obedience, according to the Words of our Saviour, *All that have heard and learn'd of the Father come to me.* He preach'd that the Death

Death of Chrift was certainly effectual for all the Elect to make
them partakers of Grace and Glory, and that it was fo far beneficial to all Men, that they are not
left in the fame defperate State
with the fallen Angels, but are
made capable of Salvation by the
Grace of the Gofpel: not capable of Efficience to convert themfelves, but as Subjects to receive
faving Grace. He did fo honour the
fincerity of God, as entirely to
believe his Will declared in his
Word: he would not interpret the,
Promifes of the Gofpel in a lefs
gracious fenfe than God intended
them: Therefore if Men finally
perifh, 'tis not for want of Mercy
in God, nor Merits in Chrift, but
for their wilfull refufing Salvation.

His Books of Practical Divinity
have been effectual for more nu-
merous Converfions of Sinners to
God,

God, than any printed in our
time: and while the Church remains on Earth, will be of continual Efficacy to recover loft
Souls. There is a vigorous Pulfe
in them that keeps the Reader a-
wake and attentive. His Book of
the *Saints Everlafting Reft*, was
written by him when languifhing
in the fufpence of Life and Death,
but has the Signatures of his holy
and vigorous Mind. To allure our
Defires, he unvails the Sanctuary
above, and difcovers the Glory and
Joys of the Bleffed in the Divine
Prefence, by a Light fo ftrong and
lively, that all the glittering Vanities of this World vanifh in that
Comparifon, and a fincere Believer
will defpife them, as one of mature
Age does the Toys and Baubles of
Children. To excite our fear he
removes the Skreen, and makes
the Everlafting Fire of Hell fo
vifible, and reprefents the tor-
menting

menting Paffions of the Damned
in thofe dreadfull Colours, that if
duly confidered, would check and
controul the unbridled licentious
Appetites of the moft fenfual
Wretches.

His *Call to the Unconverted*;
how fmall in bulk, but how powerfull in vertue ?   Truth fpeaks in
it with that authority and efficacy, that it makes the Reader to lay
his hand upon his heart, and find
he has a Soul and a Confcience,
though he lived before as if he
had none.   He told fome friends,
that fix Brothers were Converted
by reading that Call; and that e-
very Week he received Letters of
fome Converted by his Books.
This he fpake with moft humble
thankfulnefs, that God was pleafed to ufe him as an inftrument
for the Salvation of Souls.

He that was fo folicitous for the
Salvation of others, was not neg-

ligent of his own; but as regular Love requires, his firſt Care was to prepare himſelf for Heaven. In him the Vertues of the Contemplative and Active Life were eminently united. His time was ſpent in Communion with God, and in Charity to Men. He lived above the ſenſible World, and in ſolitude and ſilence convers'd with God. The frequent and ſerious Meditation of Eternal things was the powerfull means to make his Heart holy and heavenly, and from thence his Converſation. His Life was a practical Sermon, a drawing Example. There was an Air of Humility and Sanctity in his mortified Countenance; and his Deportment was becoming a Stranger upon Earth, and a Citizen of Heaven.

Though all Divine Graces, the *fruit of the Spirit*, were viſible in his Converſation, yet ſome were more eminent. Hu-

Humility is to other Graces, as the Morning-Star is to the Sun, that goes before it, and follows it in the Evening: Humility prepares us for the receiving of Grace, *God gives Grace to the humble:* and it follows the Exercife of Grace; *Not I*, fays the Apoflle, *but the Grace of God in me.* In Mr. *Baxter* there was a rare Union of fublime Knowledge, and other fpiritual Excellencies, with the loweft opinion of himfelf. He wrote to one that fent a Letter to him full of Expreffions of Honour and Efteem, *You do admire one you do not know; Knowledge will cure your Error. The more we know God, the more reafon we fee to admire him;* but our knowledge of the Creature difcovers its imperfectiohs, and leffens our efteem. To the fame perfon expreffing his Veneration of him for his excellent Gifts and Graces, he replied with

I 2   heat;

heat, *I have the remainders of pride in me, how dare you blow up the sparks of it?* He defir'd fome Minifters, his chofen friends, to meet at his Houfe, and fpend a day in Prayer for his direction in a matter of moment: before the Duty was begun, he faid, *I have defir'd your affistance at this time, becaufe I believe God will fooner hear your Prayers than mine.* He imitated St. *Auftin* both in his Penitential Confeffions, and Retractations. In conjunction with Humility, he had great Candor for others. He could willingly bear with perfons of differing Sentiments: *he would not proftitute his own judgment, nor ravifh anothers.* He did not over-efteem himfelf, nor under-value others. He would give liberal Encomiums of many Conforming Divines. He was fevere to himfelf, but candid in excufing the faults of others. Where-

as,

as, the bufie Inquirer and Cenfurer of the faults of others, is ufually the eafie Neglecter of his own.

Self-denial and Contempt of the World were fhining Graces in him. I never knew any perfon lefs indulgent to himfelf, and more indifferent to his Temporal intereft. The offer of a Bifho-prick was no temptation to him : for his exalted Soul defpifed the Pleafures and Profits which others fo earneftly defire ; he valued not an empty Title upon his Tomb.

His Patience was truly Chrifti-an. God does often try his Chil-dren by Afflictions, to exercife their Graces, to occafion their Victory, and to entitle them to a triumphant Felicity.

This Saint was tried by many Afflictions. We are very tender of our Reputation : his Name was obfcur'd under a Cloud of detrac-tion. Many flanderous Darts were

thrown at him. He was charg'd
with Schifm and Sedition. He
was accus'd for his Paraphrafe upon the New Teftament, as guilty
of difloyal Afperfions upon the
Government, and Condemn'd, un-
heard, to a Prifcn, where he remain d for fome years. But he was
fo far from being moved at the
unrighteous profecution, that he
joyfully faid to a conftant friend,
What could I defire more of God,
than after having ferv'd him to my
power, I fhould now be called to
fuffer for him. One who had Leen
a fierce Diffenter, was afterward
rankled with an oppofite heat, and
very contumelioufly in his Writings reflected upon Mr. *Baxter,*
who calmly endur'd his Contempt:
and when the fame perfon publifht
a learned Difcourfe in Defence of
Chriftianity, Mr. *Baxter* faid, *I*
forgive him all for his Writing that
Book. Indeed he was fo much the
more

more truly honourable, as he was
thought worthy of the hatred of
thofe perfons.

'Tis true, the Cenfures and Re-
proaches of others whom ·he e-
fteemed and loved, toucht him in
the tender part. But he, with the
great Apoftle, *counted it a fmall
thing to be judg'd by Mens day.* He
was entire to his Confcience, and
independent upon the opinion of·
others. But his Patience was more
eminently tried by his continual
pains and languifhing. Martyrdom
is a more eafie way of dying, when
the Combat and the Victory are
finifht at once, than to dye by degrees every day. His Complaints
were frequent, but who ever heard
an ‿ unfubmiffive word drop from
his lips ? He was not put out of
his Patience, nor out of the poffef-
fion of himfelf. In his fharp Pains,
he faid, *I have a rational Patience,
and a believing Patience,* though
fenfe would recoil.   His

His pacifick Spirit was, a clear Character of his being a Child of God. How ardently he endeavour'd to cement the breaches among us, which others widen and keep open, is publickly known. He said to a friend, *I can as willingly be a Martyr for Love, as for any Article of the Creed.* 'Tis ftrange to aftonifhment, that thofe who agree in the fubftantial and great Points of the Reformed Religion, and are of differing Sentiments onely in things not fo clear, nor of that moment as thofe wherein they confent, fhould ftill be oppofite Parties. Methinks the remembrance how our Divifions lately expos'd us to our watchfull Adverfary, and were almoft fatal to the intereft of Religion, fhould conciliate our Affections. Our common danger and common deliverance, fhould prepare our Spirits for a fincere and firm Union. When our Sky was

fo

fo dark without a glimmering Horizon, then by a new dawning of God's wonderful Providence, a Deliverer appear'd, our gracious Soveraign, who has the Honour of eftablifhing our Religion at home, and gives us hopes of reftoring it abroad, in places from whence it has been fo unrighteoufly and cruelly expell'd. May the Union of his Proteftant Subjects in religious things fo defir'd by wife and good Men, be accomplifht by his princely Counfel and Authority. Integrity with Charity would remove thofe things that have fo long difunited us. I return from this Digreffion.

Love to the Souls of Men was the peculiar Character of Mr. *Baxter's* Spirit. In this he imitated and honoured our Saviour, who prayed, dyed, and lives for the Salvation of Souls. All his natural and fupernatural Endowments

ments were fubfervient to this
bleffed End. It was *his Meat and
Drink*, the Life and Joy of his
Life to doe good to Souls. His
Induftry was almoft incredible in
his Studies: he had a fenfitive nature defirous of eafe as others have,
and faint Faculties, yet fuch was
the continual Application of himfelf to his great Work, as if the
Labour of one Day had fupplyed
ftrength for another, *and the willingnefs of the Spirit had fupported
the Weaknefs of the Flefh.* In his
ufual Converfation, his ferious,
frequent and delightfull Difcourfe
was of Divine things, to inflame
his Friends with the Love of Heaven. He received with tender
Compaffion and condefcending
Kindnefs, the meaneft that came
to him for Councel and Confola-
tion. He gave in one year a hun-
dred Pounds to buy Bibles for the
poor. He has in his Will difpos'd
of

of all that remains of his Eſtate after the Legacies to his Kindred, for the benefit of the Souls and Bodies of the Poor. He continued to preach ſo long notwithſtanding his waſted languiſhing Body, that the laſt time, he almoſt died in the Pulpit. It would have been his joy to have been *transfigured in the Mount*.

Not long after his laſt Sermon, he felt the Approaches of Death, and was confin'd to his ſick Bed. Death reveals the Secrets of the Heart, then words are ſpoken with moſt feeling and leaſt Affectation. This excellent Saint was the ſame in his Life and Death: his laſt Hours were ſpent in preparing others and himſelf to appear before God. He ſaid to his Friends that viſited him, *You come hither to learn to dye, I am not the onely Perſon that muſt go this way, I can aſſure you, that your whole Life be*

it

it never so long is little enough to prepare for Death. Have a care of this vain deceitful World, and the Lusts of the Flesh: be sure you choose God for your portion, Heaven for your home, God's Glory for your end, His word for your rule, and then you need never fear but we shall meet with Comfort.

Never was a Sinner more humble and debasing himself, never was a sincere Believer more calm and comfortable. He acknowledged himself to be the vilest Dunghil-worm ('twas his usual Expression) that ever went to Heaven. He admir'd the Divine Condescension to us, often saying, *Lord what is Man, what am I vile Worm to the great God?* Many times he prayed, *God be merciful to me a Sinner,* and blessed God, that that was left upon record in the Gospel as an effectual Prayer. He said, *God may*

may juftly condemn me for the beft Duty I ever did: and all my hopes are from the free Mercy of God in Chrift, which he often prayed for.

After a flumber he wak'd and faid, *I fhall reft from my Labour:* a Minifter then prefent faid, *And your Works follow you:* to whom he replyed, *No Works, I will leave out Works, if God will grant me the other.* When a Friend was comforting him with the remembrance of the good many had received by his preaching and Writings, he faid, *I was but a Pen in God's hand, and what praife is due to a Pen.*

His refign'd Submiffion to the Will of God in his fharp Sicknefs, was eminent. When extremity of pain conftrain'd him earneftly to pray to God for his releafe by Death, he would check himfelf; *It is not fit for me to prefcribe, and faid, when thou wilt, what thou wilt, how thou wilt.*

Be-

Being in great Anguifh, he faid, *O how unfearchable are his ways and his paths paft finding out! the reaches of his Providence we cannot fathom :* and to his Friends, *Do not think the worfe of Religion for what you fee me fuffer.*

Being often ask'd by his Friends, how it was with his inward Man, he replied, *I blefs God I have a well-grounded Affurance of my Eternal Happinefs, and great Peace and Comfort within ; but it was his trouble he could not triumphantly exprefs it, by reafon of his extreme pains.* He faid, *Flefh muft perifh, and we muft feel the perifhing of it : and that though his Judgment fubmitted, yet fenfe would ftill make him groan.*

Being asked by a Perfon of Quality, whether he had not great Joy from his believing Apprehenfions of the invifible State, he replied : *What elfe think you Chriftianity ſtianity ſerves for ?* He ſaid, *The Conſideration of the Deity in his Glory and Greatneſs was too high for our Thoughts ; but the Conſide-ration of the Son of God in our Na-ture, and of the Saints in Heaven, whom he knew and loved, did much ſweeten and familiarize Heaven to him.* The deſcription of Heaven in the 12. to the *Heb.* and the 22. was moſt comfortable to him.: *That he was going to the innumera-ble company of Angels, and to the general Aſſembly and Church of the firſt-born, whoſe Names are written in Heaven; and to God the Judge of all, and to the ſpirits of juſt men made perfeɭt ; And to Jeſus the Mediator of the new Covenant, and to the blood of ſprinkling that ſpeaks better things than the blood of Abel.* That Scripture, he ſaid, *deſerved a thouſand thouſand thoughts :* He ſaid, O *how comfor-table is that promiſe, Eye has not ſeen,*

seen, nor Ear heard, neither hath it entred into the heart of Man to conceive the things God hath laid up for those who love him.

At another time he said, *That he found great comfort and sweetneß in repeating the words of the Lord's Prayer, and was sorry that some good people were prejudiced againſt the uſe of it ; for there were all ne-ceſſary Petitions for Soul and Body contain'd in it.*

At other times he gave excellent Counſel to young Miniſters that viſited him, *and earneſtly prayed to God to bleß their labours, and make them very ſucceſsfull in Converting many Souls to Chriſt :* And exprefs'd great joy in the hopes that God would do a great deal of good by them ; and that they were of moderate peacefull Spirits.

He

He did often pray that God *would be mercifull to this misera-ble distracted World: and that he would preserve his Church and In-terest in it.*

He advis'd his Friends to *be-ware of self-conceitedness, as a Sin that was likely to ruine this Na-tion:* and said, *I have written a Book against it, which I am afraid has done little good.*

Being ask'd whether he had alter'd his mind in Controversial Points, he said, *Those that please may know my mind in my Writings: and what he had done was not for his own Reputation, but the Glory of God.*

I went to him with a very wor-thy Friend, Mr. *Mather* of *New-England,* the day before he died, and speaking some comforting Words to him, he replyed, *I have pain, there is no arguing against sense, but I have peace, I have peace.*

K   I

I told him you are now approaching to your long-defir'd home, he anfwer'd, *I believe, I believe.* He faid to Mr. *Mather, I blefs God that you have accomplifht your bufinefs, the Lord prolong your Life.*

He expreft a great willingnefs to dye, and during his Sicknefs, when the Queftion was ask'd, how he did, his reply was, *almoft well.* His joy was moft remarkable, when in his own apprehenfions; Death was neareft : and his Spiritual Joy at length was confummate in Eternal Joy.

Thus lived and dyed that blefled Saint. I have without any artificial Fiction of words, given a fincere fhort Account of him. All our Tears are below the juft grief for fuch an unvaluable Lofs. It is the Comfort of his Friends, that he enjoys a blefled Reward in Heaven, and has left a precious Remembrance on the Earth.

Now

Now bleſſed be the gracious God, that he was pleaſed to pro-long the Life of his Servant, ſo uſeful and beneficial to the World to a full Age : that he has brought him ſlowly and ſafely to Heaven. I ſhall conclude this Account with my own deliberate Wiſh : May I live the ſhort remainder of my Life, as entirely to the Glory of God, as he lived; and when I ſhall come to the Period of my Life, may I dye in the ſame bleſſed Peace wherein he died; may I be with him in the Kingdom of Light and Love for ever.

P·O S T S C R I P T.

I Shall annex two Paſſages decla-ratory, the one of his Humility, the other of his Excellent Abilities. He had ſuch an Abhorrence of him-ſelf for his Sins, that he ſaid to a Mi-niſter, *I can more eaſily believe, that*
God

God will forgive me, than I can forgive my self. The other was, being in the Pulpit to preach, he found that he had forgot to put his Notes into his Bible: he pray'd to God for his Affiftance, and took the firft Text that occurr'd to his View in opening the Bible: and preach'd an Excellent Sermon for the Matter and Order of it upon the Priefthood of Chrift. After he was come down, he enquir'd of a Minifter prefent, whether he had not tir'd him, who replyed, *No*; but with feveral others declar'd they were exceedingly fatisfied with his Difcourfe: he faid, *It was neceffary to have a Body of Divinity in ones Head.*

FINIS.

BOOKS writ by *William Bates*, D. D. and fold by *B. Aylmer*.

THE *Harmony of the Divine Attributes, in the Contrivance and Accomplifhment of Man's Redemption by the Lord Jefus Chrift*: *Or Difcourfes, wherein is fhewed, how the Wifdom Mercy, Juftice, Holinefs, Power, and Truth of God are glorified in that great and bleffed Work*, In Octavo.

Confiderations of the Exiftence of God, and of the Immortality of the Soul, with the Recompence of the Future State. To which is added the Divinity af the Chriftian Religion, proved by the Evidence of Reafon, and Divine Revelation, for the Cure of Infidelity, the Hectick Evil of the Times. In Octavo.

The

The Soveraign and Final Happiness of Man, with the effectual Means to obtain it. In Octavo.

The Four Last Things, Death and Judgment, Heaven and Hell, practically confidered and applied, in feveral Difcourfes. In Octavo, and Duodecimo.

The Danger of Profperity difcovered, in feveral Sermons, upon Prov. 1. 17. In Octavo.

The great Duty of Refignation in Times of Affliction, &c. In Octavo.

A Funeral Sermon preached upon the Death of the Reverend and Excellent Divine, Dr. Thomas Manton, *who deceafed* October 18, 1677. *To which is added, the laft publick Sermon* Dr. Manton *preached.* In Octavo.

The

The Sure Trial of Uprightness, *opened in several Sermons, upon* Psal. 18. v. 23. *In* Octavo.

A Description of the Blessed Place and State of the Saints above, in a Discourse on John 14. 2. *Preached at the Funeral of Mr.* Clarkson.

The Way to the highest Honour, on John 12. 26. *Preached at the Funeral of Dr.* Jacomb.

The Speedy Coming of Christ to Judgment, on Rev. 22. 12. *Preached at the Funeral of Mr.* Benj. Ashurst.

A Funeral Sermon for the Reverend, Holy and Excellent Divine, Mr. Richard Baxter, *who Deceased* December *the 8th.* 1691. *With an Account of his Life.*

A D-

ADVERTISEMENT.

NEwly printed, The Holy Bible, containing the Old Testament and the New : With Annotations and Parallel Scriptures. To which is annex'd, The Harmony of the Gospels : As also, the Reduction of the Jewish Weights, Coins and Measures, to our English Standards. And a Table of the Promises in Scripture. By *Samuel Clark*, Minister of the Gospel. Printed in Folio of a very fair Letter; the like never before in one Volume. Printed for *Brabazon Aylmer* in *Cornhill*.